Bob Moats

I0567955

TRICK OR TREAT MURDERS

Copyright © 2014 by Bob Moats.

Rev. 0328141105

Trick or Treat Murders

For information and address:
Magic 1 Productions
P.O. Box 524, Fraser MI 48026-0524
Website: http://murdernovels.com
Cover by Bob Moats
Photo from Fotosearch.com

Bob Moats

Other Jim Richards series books by Bob Moats

For a preview or to purchase a book, go to
http://murdernovels.com

What a few people are saying about Murder Novels by Bob Moats

Mr. Moats, I just got your novel "Classmate Murders" and have to let you know, I read it in one evening. That is the first book I have ever done that with. That was the most enjoyable book I have ever read. I just started reading e-books, and reading again, after getting my wife a Kindle. This book was my 12th, and the best. I just got Las Vegas Showgirls to (read) tomorrow evening. I look forward to reading many of your books in this series. I have been searching for an author and books that were fun, entertaining reads. Your books are just the ticket.

Regards, A new fan, Bill from South Carolina

****

Another very nice comment submitted through my website from Micki P.:

"I recently was given a kindle for my 60th birthday. The first book I downloaded was the Classmate Murders and have now read every one of the them. Today I started on the Fatal Rejection series. Thank you for the wonderful ride with Jim and Penny and all the rest of the troop. I have laughed and giggled thru the stories, my poor family gave me the strangest looks! Now I really want a little Yorkie!! Fatal Rejection so far is another great read! I will be looking out for more of Jim Richards and since you are my #1 Author, anything of yours I can find."

Extra special thanks to:

Special thanks to Val Brooks who edited this book and for her great suggestions.

Thanks to the beta readers Cindy Gross Valstad, Susan Houghton and Al Norris.

Thank you to all the people who purchased this book. I hope you enjoy it as much as I enjoyed writing it for my faithful readers.

The Jim Richards Family of Readers is listed in the back of the book.

Chapter 1

HALLOWEEN – 1999

The doorbell rang twice before the woman opened the door. She lived on a lonely stretch of road, so she was mildly surprised that there was a trick-or-treater pushing her doorbell. Her porch light was on—to signify there was candy—so she could see the creature standing alone at her door. The person, boy or girl, hard to tell she thought, stood fairly tall. She wondered if it was an over-sized child or some teenager begging for treats.

"Trick or Treat," came a voice from under the small, dirty-looking, burlap bag covering the head and tied around the person's neck. There were two small holes cut for eyes and the woman could see very dark brown, almost black, eyes from within the recesses. It was hard to tell if the voice came from a girl, or a boy just before puberty. It was high pitched and yet sounded rough.

The woman studied the costume, mostly homemade, so she assumed the person was not very

6

well off monetarily. Other than the bag covering the head, the person wore a plaid wool shirt, like a lumberjack wore, and baggy blue jeans. She noticed the person had no shoes or socks. This disturbed her as it was fairly cold for Halloween in the Vegas Valley.

"You need shoes more than candy," the woman finally said.

The person just stood waiting.

"Well, I guess if it doesn't bother you, it's none of my business."

"No, it isn't, Mrs. Hall," the bag spoke.

That shook the woman up, the person knew her name. How? Was the person a neighbor or someone from her church?

"None of your business at all, Mrs. Hall," the bag spoke again. "You don't remember where my shoes are, do you?"

"Excuse me? I don't know who you are with that bag on your head. So how would I know where your shoes are?"

"Of course you wouldn't remember accusing me of stealing Jeffery's shoes, would you?" The voice was now more threatening, almost growling. "You made me give them back to that dirty little liar."

A chill ran through the woman, hearing the menace in the voice. She searched her mind to try to remember accusing anyone of stealing anyone's shoes. She vaguely remembered her long dead son had taken a friend's shoes and she made him give them back. But this person couldn't be her son. He died a few years back from an attack by an unknown assailant and left in a drainage canal. Blow to the head the police said. She had a hard time identifying the body, it had been in water for a week. But the clothes and a wallet did help identify the boy.

"Who are you and why are you saying these things?" The woman was starting to panic. "Go away, I have no candy for you!"

"Wait, Mrs. Hall. I have to give you your trick." The person reached into the bag, pulled out a .38 handgun, and fired it into the woman's chest in a perfect shot grouping.

The woman's face contorted in shock and pain as she fell back onto the rug in the hallway. The hooded assailant put the gun back into the bag and said, "Trick or treat, Mom."

PRESENT DAY - 2013

"Now how do they know the killer said that?" I asked while sitting at my desk in my office listening to Deacon tell the story.

Deacon smiled and said. "The whole incident was caught on camera. The woman's husband was a security freak. He had cameras everywhere around the house. Luckily, they also recorded sound. The whole thing was recorded so we knew what had happened. The case was never solved, lack of evidence left at the scene."

"So, you're saying the woman's son came back from the dead to take revenge for the incident with the shoes?"

"I didn't say that. I don't believe in ghosts or zombies," he said crossing himself.

"Why did you just do that?"

"Jim, I was raised in an Italian and devout Catholic home. It's an old habit when talking about the dead." Deacon smiled.

"But you said you didn't believe in ghosts or zombies, they're undead."

Trick or Treat Murders

"The victims we have to face when we go out on a murder case are usually dead. I sometimes cross myself depending on who the vic is."

"Whatever, now back to the Trick-or-Treat Killer. There was no evidence to point to the perp?"

"Nope. Everything the recording revealed was never substantiated by the husband. He never heard about any shoe incident. He did say he couldn't identify his son's body. Too badly decomposed."

"You're thinking it might not be the son who died. That the son murdered some boy and dressed him up in his own clothes and left evidence that the body was the son. Am I right?"

"This is why I like you, Jim. You have a devious mind that gets to the point. Most times."

"Most times? When have I been wrong?" I protested.

"You really want me to list them?" he said with a grin.

I shut up.

"Halloween is in four days. Every year for the last fourteen, a woman has been shot at her door by an unknown assailant. The link between all those murders is that ballistics showed it was the same gun as the first killing."

"So this bag wearing, gun-toting, killer is celebrating Halloween by shooting women? Why haven't I heard warnings about this? I'm surprised that the city fathers haven't banned trick-or-treating."

"Oh, they talked about it, but Halloween in Vegas isn't something they can control. LVPD puts out more cars on the streets, but we don't have enough men to cover every street in the city. They did issue warnings on all the news stations, but that one murder always slips through."

"Same gun every year, huh? How many moms does this dead boy have?" I asked.

"We haven't been able to find a connection between all the dead women, except they've all been murdered on Halloween. None of them knew each other, they didn't go to the same church, nor were they in any social clubs together. A couple of them had gambling problems, but that's hardly a cause to murder them. So, we are on high alert to keep one woman from dying this year, as we have been for the last twelve years, when we realized the pattern of the crimes."

"Well, I don't envy you this job. With thousands of people walking around in disguises, how do you land one bad guy, or ghost? Maybe you can call those paranormal ghost hunters from the TV." I chuckled.

Trick or Treat Murders

"That suggestion got laughed down two years ago. We don't even bring it up anymore. It's believed that the original killer is still doing this every year. If he was the boy who the Halls said was their dead son, he'd be around twenty-eight now. I believe that's what happened, he's still out there."

"Well, if he's killing in Vegas, then he must still live here. I'd say he was a very patient serial killer. Are you going to let a fourteen year murder spree go without an investigation?"

"I was hoping you'd say that," Deacon said with a big grin.

"Oh, sure, stick this on me. Your people couldn't investigate their way out of a paper bag. Besides, I just got out of a leg cast and I'm barely able to walk straight and you want me to investigate a creepy dead kid murdering his mother over and over."

"I knew you'd love the idea."

I sat staring at my friend. "I'll need to see the original recording of the first kill."

Deacon handed me a flashdrive. I laughed, "You were pretty sure of yourself."

He smiled and said, "I read you like one of your books."

Chapter 2

"Okay, I'll give it a look. No guarantees. Who's going to pay for this if I solve the case?" I said with a smile.

"I'll pad the cost into my budget. Let me know if you need anything further," he said as he stood. "I have to get back to playing detective. Weber is on my ass ever since the kennel murders. He thinks I can solve any crime now. I don't dare disappoint him. He gave me the position in homicide when they wanted to ship me over to vice. I was surprised he kept me there."

"Weber knows you're an asset to the team. I'll study this and get back to you." I said as he headed out of my office. I reached over and turned on my computer and plugged in the flashdrive, then hit the video player icon. The video started and it was a very good image. This guy must have paid a fortune for the security cameras, the resolution was excellent. I sat and watched the crime being committed. That poor woman had no idea what was going to happen. Murder makes me sad. To think someone has lost their life so ruthlessly and it's such a waste. I hated to see people die, maybe that was why I was in this business. To bring justice for the victim.

13

Trick or Treat Murders

I winced when the kid shot the woman. She went down and the kid put the gun back in the bag. The video continued for about five minutes when two small children dressed as Raggedy Ann and Andy came to the door. They stood looking at the woman on the floor bleeding out. They didn't react.

I could hear a voice in the background yelling, "Say trick-or-treat!"

The girl looked to the boy and said, "This isn't even a good dead body. When is she going to jump up and scream?"

I saw a woman coming up the steps to the door and ask, "What's going on?" I presumed she was their mother.

The children pointed to the body and the woman stood long enough, waiting for the body to move, it didn't. She pulled her children away from the door. She told them to stay on the lawn as she pulled her cell phone.

I fast forwarded the video and watched as the police arrived about ten minutes later. The mother had put her children in her car and was talking to one of the officers. I couldn't hear what they were saying out on the lawn, but could guess what was being said.

The video kept playing up to where the coroner

came in to examine the body. I watched them bag her and take her out as the forensic team checked around the porch and door. Some man came in and was in a panic after talking to a detective. I presumed it was the victim's husband. They talked briefly and then the man pointed to the camera. The video ended around that time.

I didn't know if the police had stopped the video at that point or if the equipment stopped on its own. Most security cameras have motion sensors, and at that point there was so much movement, it had to have been shut off by the police. I restarted the video at the beginning to watch it again. When it got to the shooting part, I jumped, not from the shooting, but from the voice behind me.

"That's awful. What movie is this? I'm not going to watch this on Halloween," Penny said.

I shut off the video and stood. I went around the desk to her and said, "That wasn't a Hollywood movie babe, that's a video from a security camera that caught a murder fourteen years ago."

"You're telling me I watched a real murder happen?"

"Yep, this shouldn't bother you. You've shot a couple people dead yourself."

"Not deliberately. That was in self-defense. This

15

was a brutal murder. Have they caught the killer?"

"No, it's sort of a cold case. I was asked to look into it."

"Sort of a cold case? What's that mean?" She moved closer to me, asking.

"That case didn't end there. Every year for the last fourteen, a woman has been murdered standing at her door on Halloween. The same gun was used in every shooting."

"The killer must have taken good care of the gun to last that long. Why were you asked to work on this case?"

"Deacon just wanted me to take a look at the evidence. Maybe I'd see something."

"Something that, after all these years, the police couldn't deduce?"

"This is a big deal to the police, but the killer has been very cautious in not leaving any trace."

"So what are they doing about this? Halloween is in four days, and Devil's Night in three."

"All they can possibly do. I'm sure the police don't need any more women dying. Now what are you doing here so early?"

"Early? It's almost noon. What time zone are you in?"

I looked at my watch and realized I zipped through the morning without noticing. I hated when that happened. "So, have you had lunch yet?"

"Nice segue into changing the subject. Yes, I'm up for food. Can you eat after watching that murder?" she asked.

"I have a strong stomach," I said.

"Yes, because there is so much of it," she replied with a laugh.

"Okay, enough of the beer gut jokes. I'm not ashamed of my…well, maybe a little."

"Fine, I'll go find the dog and we can go eat. NO fast food. A nice sit down lunch."

She breezed out of my office to look for Willy, our Yorkie. I could still smell her perfume. She never went out without spritzing her favorite perfume. One of the many things I loved about her. She was very feminine. I'm not talking radical feminism, like some of the bra burners of the 60's. I'm talking feminine, like skirts and make-up and perfume. She rarely, if ever, wore slacks or jeans, she knew she had great legs and liked to show them in a skirt or shorts. A real lady, she was.

I made sure my computer was off and went out to the lobby. Lacey was standing talking to Penny as I came through the glass doors. They both looked at me and giggled.

"What? Is my fly open?" I checked myself. I was zipped up.

"No sweetie, we were discussing your leg cast. The one we hung on the wall in the lounge."

"You hung my cast on the wall?" I asked, not realizing they had. I went around the counter to the door going to Lynn and Buck's offices and our lounge. I opened the lounge door and there it was. My leg cast that the doctors removed about a month ago, like a stuffed fish caught and mounted.

It looked strange and I laughed. "Why did you do this?" I asked.

"You had so many people sign it, some celebrities and headliners on the strip. It's a keepsake."

"Yes, and a reminder of my suffering through the whole ordeal." I paused. "But you are right, it does have a number of famous people all wishing me well. Okay, I'll accept this. Maybe I'll move the bullets and the mementos of my beating death that I have on my office wall next to the cast. Make it my trophy wall."

Penny laughed and said, "Let's go eat, please. You can reminisce later."

We went back to the lobby and I told Lacey to hold my calls. I was expecting her to make a silly comment about no one ever calling me, but she didn't. She gave me a sad look. I stopped.

"Lacey, what's the matter? Talk to me."

She looked up and sighed. "It's Jessie, I think she's getting herself into trouble."

*

Chapter 3

I looked to Penny. She had a concerned expression and said, "Lacey, what's wrong with Jessie?"

Jessie was the young girl orphaned when her abusive father was murdered by the Vegas Vigilante. Penny and I watched over her at our home until Lacey and Mac got married shortly after, and they became her foster parents. She'd been living with them ever since and as far as I knew, it was a happy home.

I went around the counter to her and sat on the chair next to her desk. "Talk to us, Lacey. We're as concerned about Jessie as you are."

She looked distressed, and then Penny came around to her. "Please talk to us, Lacey.

Lacey finally said, "I didn't want to upset you guys," she paused. "I was getting her gym clothes to wash and I found a cell phone in her bag. We never gave her a cell phone. She's too young to have one. Besides, I felt it would interfere with her grades. I was afraid she'd spend too much time on it and not concentrating on her school work. We told her if she maintained an 'A' average this year, we'd consider getting her one."

"Kids nowadays need them for security, besides texting their friends. How do you feel she's getting in trouble by having a cell phone that you didn't give her?" I asked.

"I went through it and found pictures of young girls and boys. They look like they were drinking and smoking...well, pot. There were no pictures of Jessie, but she had to be the person taking the pictures."

"Lacey, are you sure it was Jessie's phone?" Penny asked.

"I didn't see anything that said it was, but why did she have it?"

"Where is the phone now?" I asked.

Lacey leaned down and picked up her purse. She reached in and took out the phone. She handed it to me, I looked it over. "What do you know about Android phones?" I asked.

"Not much, but I did find the photos." She replied.

I played with it while Penny and Lacey watched. I pulled up the text messaging program and scrolled through the texts. "Who's Laurie?" I asked Lacey.

She thought for a moment and then said, "I think she's one of Jessie's friends. Laurie Evert. Why?"

"Well, all of these texts are to and from someone named Laurie, not Jessie. This Laurie talks about the parties they are having after school. I don't see Jessie's name mentioned anywhere. Wait, here it is." I was quiet as I read the text. Then I read out loud, "Mike, I talked to Jessie and she'll be my excuse for not coming home tonight. She's not happy about lying for me, but she will do it if asked." I looked to Lacey. "Well, it seems this phone isn't Jessie's. Why she had it, I can't say. But she was helping a friend, and it seems she's not into these parties."

Lacey took a breath and smiled as I said, "Now you have to explain to Jessie why you have the phone."

"She won't know until tomorrow. Her gym bag isn't needed until then. I'll put it back before she finds it missing."

"Maybe you should confront her about finding it and be understanding," I said. "Let her know you know. Just so she doesn't think she is getting away with something. Talk to her, and not as a nagging mother."

Penny said, "Jim's right. Connect with her and let her know you aren't upset. It will just upset her."

"Thanks, guys. Sorry to keep you from your lunch."

"You and Jessie are more important to us than a lunch. I can order out for a pizza, but I can't order out for a friend." I said.

Lacey was trying not to tear up. She stood and said, "Sorry, I have to use the ladies' room." She went off.

"I think we need to order in," I said. "How about some nice Italian take-out from Angelo's? Enough for all of us."

Penny kissed the top of my head and said, "I think that's the best lunch we could have today. Are you going to call?"

"I will," I said and went to my office.

An hour later, Angelo and two of his employees were standing in our lounge with heaps of food. "Angelo, you outdid yourself. I didn't order all this food."

"Hey, Mr. R, you is a good friend. I take care of my friends," he said, his accent reverting back to his days as a 'leg breaker' for the mob.

"Well, it's appreciated. I need to get whoever else is in the building to join us. No sense wasting all this food. Be right back." I went out.

"So Angelo, how are you and Sophia getting along?" Penny asked as she heaped food on her plate.

"We're solid, Mrs. R, she's a great lady. We have so much fun together. I really like her." Angelo said with a big grin.

"Well, that's a beginning. You two have been together for a couple months now, right?"

"Three months tomorrow," he said, busting with pride.

"Stay happy then, my friend," Penny said.

"I plan on it." He grinned again.

~~*~~

"Hey, Jeffery," the voice came from across the room. The man at the desk looked startled and turned to the voice. He squinted his failing eyes at the stranger, but couldn't place him. The unknown man moved around the rows of desks in the now empty office that would normally have more people at phones making cold calls, all trying to sell life insurance. It was the end of the day and Jeffery was still there alone.

"Do I know you?" Jeffery asked of the man approaching.

"Sure you do Jeffie, I'm your old buddy, Tony."

The man at the desk suddenly took on a surprised expression.

"Tony? But you can't be Tony, he died years ago."

"No, Jeff, I'm his ghost and I've returned to take my shoes back. The ones you lied to my mother about. The ones you said were yours. You knew my mother never paid attention to my things. Those new Reeboks were my shoes, but you told my mother that I took them from you. Dirty little liar. She made me give them to you. I want them back."

"Tony, be reasonable. I don't have them anymore. How is it you're still alive? I went to your funeral."

"You even wore my shoes at the funeral to wish me well into the afterlife. I know because I watched them bury me. You had the nerve to wear them, you son-of-a-bitch."

"Tony, I said I don't have them." Jeff said, starting to get nervous. "I'll be glad to pay you for them. How much do you want?"

"Well, that's interesting. Let's see, interest over fourteen years could come to a hefty sum, Jeff. How much money do you have in your account?"

"I'm not sure, I'm not rich. Hey, I sell life insurance. I don't make much in commissions."

"Well, you better come up with a good sum. I'll be watching you closely." He pulled back his jacket and showed Jeff the .38 caliber gun he had in his belt. "Don't even attempt to contact the police. I'll take you out like I did that kid they thought was me back when I died. He was a homeless kid, my age and build. I hit him with a baseball bat and then switched clothes with him. I figured his body in that drainage canal would be pretty decomposed after a while. I'll do the same to you, Jeff. So don't fuck with me."

*

Chapter 4

Jeff was trying not to piss his pants. "I won't say a word, Tony. Really, I won't."

"Better not. As I said, I'll be watching you. I got all the time in the world." He laughed and left the office.

Jeff reached for the phone and started to dial. He heard the voice again.

"Don't do it, Jeff. I said I'll be watching." Tony said from the corner of the wall by the exit. He pulled his gun, aimed and said, "Bang."

Jeff hung up and held his hands in the air.

"Good boy, now get my money," Tony said and disappeared around the corner.

Bob Moats

~~*~~

"Excellent food, Angelo," Lynn said as she wolfed down the last cannoli. Everyone was enjoying the feast that Angelo and his people had brought.

"Thanks, I have good people working for me who put their heart and soul into our food." Angelo replied. "Including Jim's daughter," he said, looking over to me playing the pinball machine I bought for the lounge. I loved pinball and this was an older machine. It brought back memories of days spent playing the machines in my favorite hangout.

"Thanks Angelo, I'm proud of her. I'm glad she's doing well for you," I said back to him, as the little silver ball binged and popped around the machine and lit up the board with every crash into the sides and bumpers. Then I lost the last ball down the hole. Story of my life.

I went over to Penny who was standing by Trapper, both munching on the appetizers. "Now I have to save Halloween." I said.

Buck was standing behind me with Earl and said, "Halloween? How are you going to save it?"

I explained to everyone in the room what Deacon had told me.

Trick or Treat Murders

"I remember that case." Lynn said. "I was just a rookie on Metro police when they were trying to find the perp just after Halloween of that year. 1999, I think it was. It's a crap shoot to find one killer in a costume out of thousands of partiers. No amount of cameras on or off the strip could keep track of one disguised person. It's worse than Mardi Gras here at Halloween. Not everyone dresses, of course. Just the locals, and they go to the many haunted houses set up. After they get bored with that they head out to the strip."

"Not to mention the thousands of children trick-or-treating in the subdivisions around the city." Lacey added. "I have to admit, I used to dress up even when I was in my late teens. I could hit two subs in one night and come home with a ton of candy."

"Back in Detroit, for a while, they had bad candy being given out— needles in apples, candy poisoned. Not a fun time," I said.

"That's just plain sadistic," Lynn said. "I'd like to get my hands on anyone who'd stick a needle in a child's apple."

"Well, that stuff stopped because everyone was getting vigilant about checking their kid's candy. Some mothers even took the addresses down of each house they visited and put the candy in small labeled bags to check later. The police were offering to use their metal detectors on the candy to be sure it was safe. Now here's some person out there murdering one woman each year giving out candy."

Penny said, "But you'll stop him, won't you?"

"Why haven't all the LVPD detectives and police been able to stop him in fourteen years?" Buck asked.

"Because he hits and runs. Only one kill and gone." I said. "No pattern or motive. He doesn't hide the body or clean up the crime scene, just shoots and walks away. He's a serial killer with a patient agenda."

"It's amazing that they got the original shooting on video," Earl said. "I'd like to see it."

"You love all that horrible stuff, Earl," Penny said.

"This intrigues me. I'd like to help if you don't mind?"

I smiled and said, "You sure can."

"Of course, Jim can sit back and take all the credit for your work, Earl," Lynn said.

"Hey, I do work hard." I defended.

Penny kissed me and said, "We know you do, sweetie."

Angelo and his people were gathering all the trays and dishes to take back to the restaurant. I went to him and said, "So, what's the damage?"

"Not a thing, Mr. R, it's on the house." He replied, showing his toothy smile.

"Angelo, you can't keep giving away food. Especially this amount."

"I don't mind. I'm planning on getting into catering also. So this was a practice run for a small party. It helps me to work out the logistics."

Logistics, I thought. Angelo was working on his vocabulary. "Well, I'll be the first to give you a great reference for future clients. That was perfect."

I could tell Angelo was proud of his work, I was happy for him to have come so far from the mob life to establish himself as a restaurateur.

He gathered the last of the equipment and they were gone. Everyone was filled and happy.

"All this good food, now let's not get lazy today." I said.

Lacey said, "Are you going into your office now, to meditate?"

I laughed and said, "No, I have to save Halloween."

~~*~~

Jeffrey Lowbrill left his office and hurried to his car in the almost empty parking structure. He got in and threw his briefcase on the passenger seat. He put the key in the ignition, glanced in the rearview mirror and had a shock. He saw Tony grinning at him from his back seat.

He turned his head to the back and said, "Tony, what are you doing in my car?"

"Keeping up with my plan, Jeff. Now drive where I tell you to go. Move!" Tony yelled holding the gun at Jeff's head.

He started the car and pulled out of the parking structure. Tony gave him directions out of the city and down to an area about five miles south out of the city that was quite secluded. He told Jeff to park in an area that was mostly desert for miles around. Tony had him shut off the car and got out.

31

Trick or Treat Murders

"Don't sit there. Get out!" Tony yelled and stood back, still holding the gun.

"Tony, you aren't going to shoot me, are you?" Jeff said, his voice cracking.

"Take off your shoes." Tony spoke softly.

Jeff quickly pulled the shoes from his feet. He handed them to Tony and asked, "Do I still have to pay you back?"

"No, Jeff. I decided to let the money go. I have all I need to live on, except you don't need to live."

He raised the gun and fired twice. Jeff fell to the ground.

Jeff looked up and with gasping breath said, "Why now?"

Tony bent down to him and said, "I was twelve when I made my first kill of that homeless kid. I was fourteen when I did my mother in, and every mother after that who needed to be killed. It's fourteen Halloweens later, and I wanted to kill someone from my past who also did me wrong. You came to mind. I let you go all these years, but it's time to collect. Sorry, old buddy."

Jeff closed his eyes, coughed and let out his last breath.

"I have one more to eliminate, then I'll rest. Happy Halloween, Jeffrey."

*

Chapter 5

Everyone wandered back to their offices, while Penny went with Lacey and Tracey back to the front. I went to the storeroom where Buck recently had his office, before I had the addition built. I pulled out the stand-up dry erase board that I hardly used and rolled it to my office. I suddenly felt the presence of someone behind me. I thought it might be Penny, it turned out to be Earl.

"Can I watch the video?" he asked.

I held in a laugh and said, "Sure, sit next to my desk and I'll start it for you."

I went to my desk and played the video as Earl sat watching. I pulled the board over and placed it across from my desk so I could see it when I sat. I went to a drawer in my desk and pulled out a large map of the surrounding area of Vegas. I picked up the tape and opened the map, taping it to the wall next to the board. I was now set to investigate the Trick-or-Treat Killer.

I went back around Earl to my seat and sat down. The video had gone past the shooting and was now into the husband fussing about his wife. Then the video ended.

"We need to talk to the husband." Earl said, as I shut off the video player.

"Fourteen years later, you think he's going to remember anything?"

"Grieving husbands never forget. If it weren't for the continuity of the killings every year, I'd say he could have been behind it. But I'd still like to talk to him."

"I have to call Deacon for a few things I thought of that will help me set up my board. We don't have much to go on other than that video. I'm certain the kid didn't die and he murdered his mother."

"How are you going to prove it?" Earl said.

"I need to see the boy's autopsy report, if there was one. Maybe since the parents identified the body, they didn't do a thorough examination of the body. If I can get his dental records and have the body exhumed, we can prove it's not the kid buried there."

34

"Then you're going to have to talk to the father. Like I said. You'll need his permission to dig up the kid."

"You know as much as I do about this, so can you go talk to him and see if he's agreeable? I need to coordinate with Deacon."

"I'll need an address."

"Okay, you'll have to wait while I get the info from Deacon." I said with a grin.

"Did someone mention my name?" Came a voice from out in the hall. Deacon came around the corner of my door with a box. "I figured you'd want to see these," he said, putting the box on my desk. "Hey, Earl. How's it going?"

"Good, how's life in homicide?"

"It's a dying business," Deacon said with a big laugh.

"You're sick. What's all this?" I asked.

Deacon took the box top off and pulled out a stack of files. "Fifteen case files that I liberated from homicide storage. I figured you'd want to check them out. All the trick-or-treat murders from the last fourteen years, plus the kid's file."

Trick or Treat Murders

"Well, this is perfect. I have my crime board ready to put up the info. Earl needs the location of Mr. Hall. I'd like to exhume the son's body."

"You'll need an exhumation license for that. If this pertains to the trick-or-treat killer, I'm sure Weber can start the ball rolling. Plus you will need permission from the father, since the mother is dead. Why do you want to exhume the boy?"

"To check his dental records to be sure they buried the right boy. I think the kid is still alive." I said, looking at the case files in front of me. I found the one marked 'Anthony Hall'. I opened it and read through the coroner's report. "It says here that the boy was identified by the parents. No further examination was performed. Sloppy work for a body so decomposed."

"Back then they had a coroner who wasn't really that involved. He didn't last long from what I heard."

"Well, I'd like to have Joe Lang check the body," I said, referring to the current Clark County Medical Examiner.

"I'll warn Joe and talk to Weber. Have fun going through this mess. The father's recent address is in the kid's folder. I added it in case you needed it." I thanked him, then he turned and went out.

"Here's the address. Go talk to the man and see

36

if you can convince him to let us dig up his son, or whoever is buried there. Give him reason to doubt it's his son in the grave. We need to prove it."

"Never a pleasant thing to have to do. I'll do my best to be friendly." He stood and went out.

I started with the first murder, the boy's. I noted where they found the body from the information in the file and went to my map to locate the place. I found it and drew a circle around the area. I went back to the files, they were in chronological order, and so I pulled the next. It was the mother, Mrs. Hall. I got the address of the house they had lived in. I noted it was different from where Hall was living now. He probably moved to get away from the memories. I circled the location on the map and wrote the name next to it with a number corresponding to the first kill. I did this for all the murders, with names and putting them in numerical order.

I was looking at the map when Penny walked in. She stood next to me and studied the map too, saying nothing.

"Okay, what are we looking at?" she finally asked.

"The locations of all the yearly Halloween murders."

She was quiet again then said, "They're all in a circular pattern. Around that area over past the strip."

She was right, they all did seem to be in the same area, but spread out a bit. I wondered if the police had seen this pattern. I was sure they had. What did it mean?

"I notice that the boy was found in a drainage canal in the center of the circle. They have those to run the flood waters off when it rains here. The murders each seem to occur near the canal. Maybe something, but I don't know what." I turned to Penny and said. "I'm tired and didn't get to rest today. Shall we go home and cuddle?"

"Cuddle? You won't get any rest if you want to cuddle."

"Exactly." I smiled.

~~*~~

Earl walked up the front sidewalk to the apartment building. He found the address where Hall now lived. He knocked on the door and waited. He knocked again and then the door opened. The man standing there looked like he was a bum. He needed a shave and his clothes were raggedy.

"What do you want? You better not be selling anything," he said, his breath smelling of alcohol.

"Mr. Hall, I'm Earl Daws from Richards Investigations, I need to talk to you about something important."

"Investigations? Are you a cop?"

"No, I'm a private investigator. I'm helping the police find the person who may have killed your wife and thirteen other women over the past fourteen years. May we talk?"

"The police haven't found my wife's killer, what makes you think you can?"

"I'm persistent," Earl said with a smile.

*

Chapter 6

Hall stood looking at Earl. He was having trouble getting the words out. "What good will it do Arlene now? After all these years my wife has been gone."

"We can't do much for her, but we need to find the killer before he strikes again. It will be Halloween in four days and some woman out there will die, like your wife did."

"Why? Why are they dying?"

"That's what I'm trying to find out. Hopefully we can prevent another woman from being killed."

"What does that have to do with me?" he asked.

"Can we sit and talk? How about the bench out here," Earl said, pointing to a bench next to the door.

The man staggered out of the apartment to the bench and sat hard. He sat in the middle, so there wasn't any room for Earl. So, Earl just stood in front of the man.

"Mr. Hall, we need to find a person who may be a killer, and we have suspicions of who that person may be. But we can't identify the person without doing something that we don't want to do, but it's necessary. Have you heard of the Trick-or-Treat Killer?"

"Sure, I heard of him, the police have asked me many times if I knew anything about him. They say he murdered my wife and has murdered a number of other women. You think you know who he is?"

"We suspect someone, but we need your help to identify him."

"My help? What the hell can I do to help?"

"We need your permission to exhume your son's remains."

"Exhume. What the hell does that mean?"

Earl had hoped the man wouldn't be so drunk to not know what he meant. "It means that we need to dig up your son's remains so we can do a dental comparison."

"What?!" The man came up from the bench and moved towards Earl. Earl wasn't worried, he could take the man easily enough. The man stopped short of Earl and waited for an answer.

Earl paused, thinking about what to say so he wouldn't upset the man further. "We suspect that your son isn't dead and the only way to prove it is to check his dental records against the body in the grave. But we need your permission."

"What if I don't give it?" he asked, swaying slightly.

"Well, Mr. Hall, it would be a matter of finding a judge to sign the papers to exhume the body without your permission."

"Then why are you asking me?"

Trick or Treat Murders

"Because if you refuse to allow us to exhume your son, it would take too long to go through the procedure and we only have four days before the next woman is killed. You'd make it so much easier for us to investigate. Perhaps we can track down the killer and stop another senseless murder."

"Why do you think it's not my son in the grave?"

"Just a hunch, and something the killer said in the video when he murdered your wife."

"Is that the thing about the shoes?"

"You remember that? Do you remember him calling your wife, 'mom'?"

"I only saw the video once and I wasn't paying much attention. The shock of it all." Hall said sadly.

"Do you remember when you had to identify your son's body?" Earl asked.

The man sat back down. He stared off into the distance. "That was a blur. I couldn't believe someone just murdered him. I couldn't look at the body, it was badly decomposed. But the jacket and the clothes were his. They had a wallet from his pocket with his ID card from his school. We just figured it was him."

"What did they do with the body? Did they autopsy it?"

"No, we wanted to bury him fast. Before his body got worse. The coroner didn't argue, I think he didn't want to mess with the body. Do you really think my son is still alive? Why hasn't he contacted me?"

"This is why we need to dig him up, to be sure. If he is still alive, I haven't any idea why he hasn't contacted you. But we'd like to get this out of the way. All we need is to check the teeth in the skull against your son's dental records to see if it's him. That's all, and then we'll put the body back in the grave. Nice and peaceful like."

"If it's not my son, I don't want the body in that grave. It was supposed to be my son, not some stranger. You have my permission to dig him up. I want to know what you find out."

"You'll probably have to come in to sign some papers just to make it official, but at least we can start the procedure. Thank you Mr. Hall, and I'm sorry for your loss."

He stood and Earl shook his hand.

Before Earl left, Hall asked, "One last question, do you really think my son murdered his mother and all these other women?"

"That's what we are trying to find out."

"If my son is the Trick-or-Treat Killer, then he's still dead to me."

Earl could see a tear in his eye as he turned and went back into the apartment.

Earl felt bad putting the man through another upset, but it had to be done.

~~*~~

My cell phone buzzed and I answered. It was Earl. I put it on speaker since I was driving and then hung it in the cell phone holder.

"How did it go?" I asked.

"Actually better than I expected. He gave his permission."

"Great, I'll call Deacon and let him know. I'm heading home. I'll see you in the morning."

He agreed and I hung up. Behind me, I could see Penny in her car. At a light, I glanced quickly to the back seat where Penny put Willy. He was sleeping soundly. I was happy Earl didn't have a problem with the father. It's not a pleasant thing to dig up a long dead body, but I knew Joe Lang could handle it.

I arrived home and parked in the garage. I left the door open so Penny could pull in. I picked up Willy from the back seat and took him in the house. Penny pulled in shortly after, so I reset the driveway alarms and went to the kitchen. I put Willy down and since he already had his fill of Angelo's food, I didn't figure he'd want more. Penny came in and said, "So, do you still want to cuddle?"

I hated to turn down the offer, but I was really wearing down. "Let's just rest and see if we still want to cuddle later."

"That's fine with me," she said and went off to the bedroom.

I looked to Willy and said, "That was too easy. She's up to something." I followed her and found her in her personal bathroom getting her tub filled, already undressed and ready to soak.

"My, you are fast." I said.

"Fast and loose," she said with a smile and a wink.

~~*~~

Tony drove Jeff's car to the parking structure of the Golden Nugget. He pulled up the hoodie he wore so he wouldn't be identified on cameras. He left the car and walked the eight miles to his "home" and put the shoes and gun on a crate inside. He sat on an unmade bed and thought about what had happened that day. He was pleased. "Now to settle with one last score," he said to himself. "Then it's over."

*

Chapter 7

I woke to hear Penny already in her bathroom getting ready to go to work. My cell phone buzzed on the bedside table. I struggled to reach it and answered without looking at the ID.

"Jim, where are you?" the voice on the phone said.

I turned in bed and looked at the clock glowing in the dark room. It read 7:27. "Who is this?" I asked.

"Jim, it's Earl. I'm in the office and ready to investigate the Trick-or-Treat Killer."

46

Bob Moats

"Do you know what time it is? I don't start my day before eight. I have another half-hour to sleep and then I'll get up and come in. Until then, amuse yourself and stop calling me." I hung up.

I rolled over to try and catch the last half-hour of my normal sleeping schedule, but now I was awake. I thought about the body being dug up and it intrigued me. I sat up and swung my legs over the side of the bed. Willy was below me and ran when I planted my feet down on the floor. One day I would step on him.

I got up and went to my bathroom to get ready. I came out to find Penny just leaving.

"What? No kiss goodbye?" I said.

She kissed me, picked up Willy and laughed. Then she was out the door. I did my normal morning things and was in my car heading to the office building.

I came into my office and found Earl standing at the map on the wall. He looked over to me and said, "There's a pattern here."

"Penny saw that yesterday. They're all fairly close to each other."

"I'm surprised the cops don't concentrate on this area." Earl said.

Trick or Treat Murders

"I don't think they've connected the dots yet. I think Deacon was hoping I would. The LVPD is a busy organization, taking care of crime in a major city of this size and the amount of activities going on. I'm sure this case is a priority, but not something they can get a handle on."

"That's why they turn to us. We're the super-sleuths."

I laughed at the thought. Maybe we needed superhero costumes, but I'd look lousy in tights. "I'm sure they could figure this out. But it's like my book editors. They go through and check spelling, punctuation and grammar, but something always gets overlooked. That's why they have beta readers to double check. We are the beta readers for the police on this."

"So, do we have an exhumation license yet?"

"How should I know I just got here? I'll call Deacon and see where we are at."

"Don't bother calling, I got your permission to dig," Deacon said as he entered my office. "Mr. Hall came in early this morning and signed the permission papers to bring up the body."

"Wow, I do good work," Earl said.

"Did you threaten him or appeal to his humanity?" Deacon asked.

"I never threaten grieving fathers. I just reasoned with him."

"Well, it worked. Weber got the ball rolling and we can dig later today. Do you guys have shovels?" Deacon said, with a smile.

"I hope the cemetery has the equipment to dig up a coffin. What time?" I asked.

"Around noon. I'll come by and lead you out there. Joe Lang will be there with his men to take the coffin in to the morgue."

"Sounds pleasant. I hope this will prove fruitful. I'd hate to be wrong on this."

"Yeah, I think the father was hoping it wasn't his son in the hole." Earl said.

Deacon looked at the map on the wall. "They did something like this around the fourth year, but the kills had no pattern. Now I see they are fairly close in a circle. Amazing when you see the big picture."

"They do go around the storm drain where Anthony Hall's body was found. Almost like the ghost is reaching out from the death site." I said. Deacon crossed himself again. "Are you going to do that every time I mention death?"

"Sorry, force of habit. I have some errands to run. I found out from Hall where his son's dentist is and I called to get the dental records. Surprisingly, they still had them. I'll be back to take you out to the cemetery." He said his goodbyes and left.

"Well, we have four hours to kill, shall we go through the files of the other murder victims and see if there's a correlation?" I said.

"I love it when you use fancy words." Earl grinned.

I reached over my desk and grabbed half of the folders and handed them to him. "Start correlating."

He sat in the client chair next to my desk and opened the first file. "What are we looking for?"

"Anything. Marital status, church affiliations, kids, especially kids. They may have something to do with the younger Anthony. Back then the police figured the son was dead, so they didn't associate other children with him. May be something to look at." I went to the crime board and put up the heading 'Children' then drew a line down the board. I wrote 'Tony' in the top space.

"Okay, let's go with other kids who he may have known, maybe their mothers were his targets."

"Sounds reasonable. This first file, Karen Downs, had a son about Tony's age in school when she was murdered."

"Name and school?"

"Mark Downs, Jerome Mack Middle School."

I added that to the board. "Grab the file on the son and see what school he went to?"

Earl sorted and found the file, then opened it to read. "We have a correlation." He grinned. "Same school."

"Check the next file."

He pulled the next one from his pile and read. "Bingo! Ralph Reslen, Jerome Mack Middle School."

I wrote that on the board. "Next."

We spent the next hour checking and writing names of boys who were in Tony Hall's school.

"The police never got this because they didn't figured the son was involved. Plus the one kill per year wouldn't pop up on the whole picture. We need to call that school and get a list of all the boys in that class year and see whose mothers are still alive."

Trick or Treat Murders

"Good thinking, I'll check on the school and the mothers. You have a date with a grave," Earl said with a sly grin.

"Okay, just be subtle. You don't have a warrant, so try to polish the apple with the school."

"Matter of life or death, I'll get them to spill the info," he said and stood.

"I'll go to see Deacon and give him this news, and then he and I can go to the cemetery from there. Proving the son is still alive will make this all come together."

Earl left the building after getting the directions to the school. I took a picture with my cell phone of the crime board, now covered in names of boys who are motherless. If we could track down one or two names of mothers still alive, we'd have a chance of stopping this killer. I went to my car and drove over to see Deacon. I was happy to have some good news for him.

*

Chapter 8

Earl pulled into the parking lot of the school and could see children playing in a yard next to the building. He went in, the smell was the first thing to hit him, then the sight of all the lockers brought back memories of when he was in school. Something he didn't really want to remember. He found an adult in the hall and asked where the offices were. She pointed out the way and Earl thanked her. He read the sign on the door, it said 'Office', so it must be the place. He went up to the counter and across from him was a pleasant looking woman, perhaps in her late fifties, sitting at a desk. She looked at Earl and smiled.

"May I help you sir?" She asked.

"Is it possible to speak with the principal?"

She glanced at the open door of the principal's office and then stood. "Your name please?" she asked, and Earl told her. "Just a minute. I'll see if he's busy." She went to the office and in. A moment later she came back out and waved to Earl. "He'll see you."

Earl went through the swinging half-door of the

counter and over to the room. He thanked the woman and went in. Behind a desk was a rather large man, not overweight, but big. He was pleasant looking, so Earl hoped this would go well.

He stood and held his hand out, they shook hands, and then he said, "Mr. Daws, I'm Principal Olsen. Please sit. How may I help you?"

Earl sat and reached into his jacket pulling out his ID wallet with his P.I. license. He reached out and showed it to the principal as he spoke. "I'm a private investigator helping the LV police with a touchy problem coming up." The principal sat quietly. "Have you heard of the Trick-or-Treat Killer?"

"I have, terrible things this person has done. What does that have to do with me or my school?"

"This is going to sound crazy, but we suspect one of your past students may be the killer."

The principal's eyes widened and he leaned forward. "Why do you suspect that?"

Earl explained the story of Tony Hall possibly faking his death along with the video of killing his mother. "We are presently having his body exhumed to check his dental records to see if Tony Hall is actually buried there. The problem is, every year since Tony's mother was shot in 1999 on Halloween, a woman has died on that night. Today, my associate

54

and I determined that each of the thirteen women murdered had a son in your school at the same time Tony was enrolled here. We suspect Tony is murdering the mothers of his male classmates."

The principal let out a breath and sat back. "This is not good. What do you need from me? A list of the boys from that class maybe?"

"You should be a detective, sir. That is what we need to narrow down the list of woman who may be marked for murder on Halloween night in three days."

The principal called for the woman in the outer room. She came in. "Lily, run through the computer and get a list of all male students in the class of…" he paused and looked at Earl.

"Oh, sorry, the year would have been 1997. The year when Hall died." Earl replied.

"1997. I'll need the names of parents also. Quickly if you would."

She went off and the principal looked back to Earl. "You say that they are digging up the body of Hall?"

"Yes, sir. We hope to find that the body in the grave isn't Tony Hall. If it isn't, then he's still alive and has possibly been murdering the women."

Trick or Treat Murders

"Fourteen years? Where has he been hiding all this time?"

"If we find he's still alive, then that's the 64 thousand dollar question."

The principal laughed at the reference. "That was a lot of money back when that game show ran on TV. Now they give out millions of dollars to win on a show. Times change."

"I liked it better back then. Things were simpler. Not as many people."

"Yes, we see it in our enrollment. In 1997 even, there were less students in our classes. Now we are full to the teeth."

The secretary came back in and handed a couple sheets of paper to the principal. He studied them. "Wonderful machines, computers. They narrow down all the information one needs and so quickly. There were fourteen boys in that class, not counting Hall, he didn't graduate due to being killed. Or not."

He handed the sheets to Earl and said, "I hope this helps. Catch him before another woman is murdered."

Earl took the papers and said, "Thank you. I'm sure this will help greatly."

"Let me know what you find." The principal asked.

"I will, thanks again." He left the office and headed back out to his car. He pulled out his cell phone and made a call. "Jim, I got the list."

~~*~~

"Great. I'm with Deacon now, and we're getting ready to go to the cemetery. Why don't you meet us there?" I listened then said, "Good, see you then."

I turned to Deacon standing just outside his office door and told him about the list.

"I knew you guys could get the work done," he said with a smile.

"Sure, saves you from working. Now, I'm in no rush to go to a cemetery, but I really want to know who's in that grave."

They were about to leave when they saw Mr. Hall coming in. Deacon went to him. "Sir, why are you back here?"

"I came to find out about the body in the grave," he said quietly.

Trick or Treat Murders

"We were just on our way to the cemetery to start. Would you care to join us?"

He nodded his head. If what Earl had described was correct, then Mr. Hall had shaved and cleaned up a bit. I guess he was coming around from his despair and loss. We all went out to our cars, I wanted to take my own car, so Deacon had to ride alone, Hall followed in his.

We arrived at the cemetery and parked down by where they had buried the body of some boy, we would know if it was Tony Hall soon. Joe Lang and his men were already there with the big coroner's wagon. The cemetery had its workers out with a backhoe ready to dig.

"You really know how to spice up my day, Jim," Joe said to me.

"It's a little puzzle for you," I replied.

The cemetery workers proceeded to dig and finally got to the coffin. They carefully brought it up and Joe's men pulled it over to the large cart they brought. They disconnected the cables and wheeled it to the wagon.

"I'll have something for you shortly. I'm slow in the morgue today, so you're first in line. Besides, I know this is important, Deacon explained it to me."

Bob Moats

I said, "Thanks Joe. We'll follow you back."

The workers covered the grave with a tarp and I thought we might be putting the body back or finding the real Tony and placing him in the grave. The thought chilled me, even in the hot sun. Deacon, Hall, and I went back to our respective cars.

We all drove over to the morgue and parked in front. The wagon went to the delivery area and they unloaded the coffin. By the time we reached the autopsy room, they had the coffin in place and were working on opening it. Joe had us stay out and watch through the observation window. He put on a biohazard suit, just in case of mold or any other maladies in the sealed coffin, and sent his men out. He lifted the coffin lid, it was turned our way so we could see.

I never liked looking at decomposing bodies, so I half looked. Joe was busy examining the jaw on the skull. He held a photo copy of the dental records and examined the two.

He looked to us and his voice came through the speakers above the window. "Good news or bad, take it as you wish. This is not the body of Anthony Hall."

*

Chapter 9

My heart skipped a beat and I wanted to pump my fist and say, "Yess!"…but the father was standing next to me. So I just turned to him.

"What do you want done with the body?"

"I don't care, burn it or bury it somewhere else. I don't want it in my son's grave. I'll see my son gets put in there." He turned and left us.

I felt sorry for the man, losing a son so many years ago, then a wife. Now finding out his son is still alive, but had no contact with him in all these years. I don't think I'd be a happy man. I was surprised he didn't seem more pleased that his son wasn't dead. But he had the right to show his grief or happiness the way he wanted to.

I turned back to Earl. "Now we have to check the list you got and find out which mother is still alive."

"Mind if I join you two?" Deacon asked.

"The more minds the merrier." I said. I turned to the window as Joe was resealing the coffin and said, "Thanks Joe."

He waved back and said, "I'll give this body a thorough autopsy so whoever it is might be identified."

Deacon said, "Send the information to me, so I can send it to missing persons."

We left the morgue and drove back to my building and walked into the office. Penny was sitting at my desk watching the TV.

"Must be nice to relax while we work," I said.

She turned off the TV and stood, coming around my desk and kissed me. "Okay, you can goof around all you want." I said.

"So, what did you find out about the body in the grave?" she asked.

"It's not the son. He's still alive."

"So you think he's the killer? Hi Earl," Penny said to him as he walked in.

Earl said, "I think he's our killer. Now we have to figure out what woman he's after this year." He took the list out of his pocket and handed it to me.

I sat at my desk as Deacon entered.

Trick or Treat Murders

"Oh good, a party," Penny laughed.

"Hey, Penny. Is Lynn in?"

"No, she's out chasing some wayward wife." Penny said and sat on a chair by the crime board.

"Well, I will be busy here anyway, so it's good she's not here. I'd get distracted." He laughed and went to my desk and sat on the side chair.

Earl was behind me looking over my shoulder at the list.

"Go to the board and read off the names of the murdered women." I said to Earl. He went there and said he was ready.

He read the names as I checked off the names on the list. They were lining up. He said that was all and came back to me.

"There's one name left on the list, it would seem she is still alive. She has to be the next victim. Since this is the last name, what do you think Hall would do next year?"

Deacon's phone buzzed and he answered. He listened for a bit and then hung up. We waited.

"That was Warren, he said they found the body of some guy yesterday, out off a road south of here.

Death by gunshot, and ballistics matched it to the same gun that killed all our Halloween victims. Hall is striking out now, his MO is changing."

"Do they have an ID on the body?" Earl asked.

"Yeah, Jeffrey Lowbrill."

I looked at the list, Jeff Lowbrill's name was on it. "Here's the kicker," I said. "The last woman on the list targeted to die is Agnes Lowbrill, Jeff's mother."

"I remember in the video of the first kill, the kid in the hood said something about shoes and a kid named Jeffrey. It has to be the same person." Earl said.

"Warren did say they found him with no shoes. Maybe Hall got to him, took his shoes and murdered him."

I stood and said, "Okay, we have positive ID on the Trick-or-Treat Killer. Anthony Hall. Now we have to find him and also get protection for Agnes Lowbrill."

Deacon stood, "I'll work on the protection for Lowbrill. You can keep searching for Hall." He left the room.

Penny asked, "But where has this Hall person been hiding all these years?"

"Very good question. He murders some kid and changes identity with him, then just vanishes. In Vegas, he could hide in a lot of places. He could pick up money from tourists by robbing them, but where would he stay?"

"There are those dive motels at the north end. He could get a small apartment in one and lay low, only going out to get food or to rob someone." Earl said.

"Well, you to work it out, I'm going shopping," Penny said as she headed out. Then she stopped and said, "I'm taking Lacey with me to get Jessie some new clothes." Then she left.

"Okay, let's sit and hash out a plan," I said to Earl.

~~*~~

Penny and Lacey had just arrived at the Boulevard Mall and gone in. Penny had Willy in his purse and he was inside resting. Penny had the bag slung over her shoulder.

The two of them were down at the back end of one part of the mall when Penny was pushed and the dog purse was pulled from her shoulder. The assailant was running off with the bag as Penny was screaming for help to stop him. Lacey took off running after the man, following him down a side corridor, and then lost him somewhere in the crowd. She stood looking around as Penny came running up to Lacey.

"Son-of-a-bitch!" she yelled with tears in her eyes. "You didn't see where he went?"

"No, sorry. Everyone got in my way. He could have gone in any store and out the back way."

Penny pulled her cell phone out of her regular purse and called Deacon. He came on and Penny explained what happened. Penny pulled Lacey over to the side of a store where it was fairly quiet and turned on the speaker.

"Penny, all of our patrol cops know you and your dog. I'll get with dispatch and put out a BOLO on Willy. Can you give me a description of the perp?"

Penny was trying not to sob, she was having trouble catching her breath, so Lacey gave Deacon the description. Deacon said he'd take care of it and hung up.

"Bastard!" Penny said, crying now.

Lacey said, "I don't think the guy knew what he was taking. He'll probably get a surprise to find a dog in the bag. Maybe he'll let him loose."

Penny took a breath and said, "I hope he finds the bags of dog shit in the side pocket."

"Not much we can do now until the police find him. Let's go back to the office." Lacey said softly.

"You drive, I can't," Penny said and handed the keys to Lacey.

~~*~~

Earl and I were sorting through the files and hoping to find some connections. I sat back and said, "Now that we know it's Tony Hall committing the murders, but why go after all the mothers of his classmates?"

"Maybe he figures…Oh hell, I have no idea. I'm getting tired of sorting through all these files. Back when I was a lieutenant on the Detroit Police, I could order men to do this grunt work."

"The joys of doing it yourself as a P.I., fun huh?"

Tracey buzzed me from the front lobby, I flipped the intercom switch. "Yes, Tracey?"

"You have a call from the Las Vegas police," she said.

"Why are they calling me?"

She said, "Shouldn't you be asking them?"

I laughed and said, "Thanks Tracey, I'll get it." I hit the button to answer the phone line and put it on speaker. "Jim Richards here. May I help you?"

The voice on the phone said, "Mr. Richards, Officer Alberts here, we have your dog."

*

Chapter 10

"Are you sure? Where's my wife, she should be with the dog?" I asked.

"We got a call for a BOLO on Willy. He was taken from your wife at the Boulevard Mall. We were heading to the mall and luckily we saw a man walking down East Desert Inn Road, between Maryland and Eastern, with the dog. We stopped him and identified the dog by his collar. I presume when the collar is engraved with 'Willy Richards' then it's your dog. I didn't have your wife's number so I called your office. I'll take him and the suspect in to Deacon."

"Thank you Officer, I appreciate the call." I said and hung up.

I looked to Earl and he said, "Go rescue your dog. I'll hold down the fort."

I pulled my cell phone to call Penny just as she and Lacey were coming down the hallway. Penny was still crying. I went to her and told her they found Willy.

"Is he all right?" She sobbed.

"The officer didn't say, but I'm sure he is. They're taking him and the assailant to Deacon."

"I want a piece of him, the bastard."

"Fine, I'll see you get the best piece, now let's go."

Lacey went back to the front as we went to my car and drove over to see Deacon.

We entered the squad room and saw a number of detectives playing with Willy on a desk. He turned and saw us, his tail was wagging fast and he started barking. Penny went straight for him, picked him up and hugged him.

Deacon came out of his office and smiled. "It was really lucky that the patrol cops spotted Willy with the perp."

"Thank the officers who did and have them get ahold of me. They deserve a reward."

Penny came to us and said, "I want to see the bastard who took Willy."

Deacon smiled and led us to the holding cells. He pointed to an old man in the cell. He was dirty and had worn clothing on. He appeared to be a homeless person and looked lost.

Penny stood staring and said, "That's not the man who took Willy."

"Well, he had the dog with him," Deacon said.

"May I go in with him?" I asked.

Deacon signaled to the jailer and he unlocked the door. I went in. The old man sat just staring, then he seemed to notice me.

"Where's my dog?" he asked me in a feeble voice.

"What kind of dog was he?" I asked as I sat on the cot next to him.

Trick or Treat Murders

"Tiny, furry and cute. I found him today, but the police said I stole him. I didn't really, I found him."

He was well-wrinkled and looked to be in his seventies. His eyes were bloodshot, but I didn't think from drinking. "Where did you find the dog?"

"Behind that big store, I was looking through the dumpster and this guy came from the side and he was swearing. He ran off and the doggy came around the corner to me. I found him, I didn't steal him."

"What's your name?"

He seemed to be thinking for a moment and then said, "Fred."

"Well, Fred, I believe you when you say you didn't steal him. But the dog belongs to my wife and me." I said pointing to Penny holding Willy.

The old man looked up and frowned. "He's not my dog?"

"I'm sorry, he's not. But if you promise to take care of a dog, I'll see if we can get you one."

"That would be so nice. I have no friends and I thought the dog was a present from Heaven."

"You wait here and I'll arrange it." I stood and

went out to Deacon. "He didn't do anything but find Willy. I'll take him and see what we can do for him."

"He had no ID, so I figure he's homeless. One of hundreds roaming around the city."

"I've seen them sleeping by the streets and in culverts. I really hate the fate they were given. Maybe we can save this one."

"You can take him, we didn't book him or anything. He's free to go."

I went back in and said, "Come on Fred, we're going to get you a dog."

He had trouble standing and was slightly bent over. I helped him out of the cell as Penny was watching him. "I don't suppose you're going to put him up in our guesthouse." She smiled.

"No, I'll check with one of the shelters in town, see what they can do for him." We took him out to the car and I drove over to an animal shelter I knew of to find a small dog. His eyes lit up when he saw all the animals. He finally picked out a small mutt that didn't look like it would get very big.

Back in the car, Willy was overjoyed seeing the other pup. The old man was holding him close and the dog didn't mind, he looked happy.

Trick or Treat Murders

I drove to the office building and we went to the back door. "Am I allowed to go in there?" the old man asked.

"Sure, Fred, it's my building. You can come in."

I took him to my office as Penny went to the front to let Lacey know she had Willy. Earl was still at the desk going through files. He looked up in surprise and stood.

"Earl, this is Fred. He rescued Willy from a purse snatcher."

"Good work Fred, I'm Earl." He held his hand out to shake. The old man looked apprehensive then took Earl's hand.

I led Fred to a chair by the wall and said, "Rest here. Have you eaten today?"

He said quietly, "No."

"Okay, wait here." I went out and to Buck's office, he was going over some paperwork. I explained everything to him and he followed me back to my office.

Fred's eyes went wide when he saw the big man. "Fred, this is Buck. He's going to take you to our break room and feed you. It's good Italian food. Mostly leftovers, but still good." I turned to Buck and said to warm his food in the microwave.

Buck helped the man up and said, "Nice dog."

"He's my dog. I got him from a place where they had lots of dogs."

"That's nice," Buck said with a smile as they went out.

"Now we have to get back to our problem. I forgot to ask Deacon if they managed to find Mrs. Lowbrill." I went to my desk and picked up the phone.

After a brief conversation I hung up. "Deacon said they did contact Lowbrill and had to tell her about her son. Then to make matters worse, they explained how Hall may be coming after her. Deacon put some men on watch at her house. This may scare Hall away, but I feel he's going to try and still murder her. He didn't go to all this trouble to murder her son and not get to her."

"Well, we still need to find him, where do we start? He's been off the grid for all these years, hiding somewhere in Vegas." Earl said.

Buck came back in the room and said, "Fred's enjoying a nice warm meal. He told me something I didn't know about. He lives in tunnels under the city."

"Yeah, they're part of the Vegas flood-control system." I said. "As you know, it can rain here pretty hard, and in the desert, the rain has nowhere to go, so to prevent flooding they have the tunnels. The tunnels feed the rain out towards Lake Mead."

"He said there's hundreds of people living down there. Most are trying to stay away from the people above. They live down there all the time."

I looked to Earl and said, "Perfect place to hide. I wonder if our suspect may be a resident of the underworld?"

*

Chapter 11

We went to the lounge where we found Fred eating his food at a table. The dog was on the floor eating from a paper plate.

"Thank you, Mr. Richards, for the food, and the dog," he said smiling.

"My pleasure, now you can pay us back by helping us find someone." I said.

"I'll be glad to, what do you need to know?" He sounded a little more active, maybe the food was helping to give him some energy.

"You told Buck that you live in the storm tunnels."

"I do."

"How long have you been down there?"

He thought for a moment, then said, "Eight, maybe ten winters. I don't have any way of telling exact time."

"So that would be about ten years at the most. How have you survived so long?"

"I'm just careful and cautious. I'm set up in one of the tunnels that isn't being used by too many people. Once I was set up, others left me alone. I have to be aware of storms coming in. If I hear a warning signal, I pack quickly and get out until the flood water passes."

"Warning signal?"

"Sure, there are people I call friendlies who watch after us and they keep track of the weather. When a storm comes up, they signal through the tunnel. Word travels fast among the people down there. I've known of a few people who drown down there from not getting out in time. The water can rise fast and one could drown easily."

I was amazed. I had heard about the tunnels and the people who lived there, but never had it come to me this close. If Hall was down there, it would be a task to find him.

"How far do the tunnels go?" Earl asked.

The man looked at Earl and said, "One of the friendlies said there are about 500 miles of tunnels."

That took me by surprise. With all those tunnels, I was amazed that Vegas didn't drop into one big sinkhole. "Have you ever heard of a young man named Tony Hall?"

"I know a couple of Tonys, but they are both old, like me. People aren't real friendly down there. There are people who would beat you for your food or light. I have a crowbar that I use for protection. If someone comes through my tunnel, I have the bar in hand."

I looked at Earl and then Buck and said, "Feel like a little trip into the bowels of Vegas?"

"You thinking of going down there? You better take me or you'll get lost." Fred said.

I grinned and said, "Looks like we have a travel guide. I'll call Deacon and get a protective detail."

I went out of the lounge and into my office. I called Deacon and explained the situation. He said he'd send a car out with two of his biggest men.

I went back to the lounge and over to Fred. "Fred, how did you manage to live down there, where did you get your food?"

"There are plenty of dumpsters behind the hotels with food from their restaurants. Good food they just throw out."

"What about light? It has to be pitch black down there."

"It is. I have one of those crank lights. I keep it charged up by cranking the handle. Others use candles they get from the dollar stores."

"How do you buy things, where do you get money? You don't rob people do you?"

"Oh, my goodness no. There are many ways to get money. If one cleans up a bit and goes into the casinos, a person could make a good deal of money when people walk away from their slot machines before a payout finishes, and some leave chips or coins behind. I've come out of a casino with a couple hundred dollars in a day. I use it to buy supplies to live. Like my crank light. I also share with a few people I like."

"Okay, we have some officers coming with us for protection and we will go down into the tunnels to see what the story is. Maybe we'll get lucky and find Hall."

"Just watch yourself. Even with the police, they can get violent down there." Fred said.

Earl looked at Buck and smiled. "Are you worried?"

"Hell, no, I'd like to see some action," Buck said with a laugh.

Lacey came in and said, "There are two huge police officers in the lobby. They frighten me."

I went to Lacey, "They're on our side, don't worry. You can wait here until we've gone."

"No. I can take it. Penny told me to tell you she was going home," she said and left the lounge.

"Well, men, shall we go?" Fred had already finished his food and picked up the dog. We went out to the lobby and found that Lacey was right, the cops were huge. One was a tremendously big black officer. He looked like a linebacker for the Rams. The other white officer could bench press a Volkswagen. "Welcome men," I said and explained to them what was happening.

The black cop said, "I went down there once before when we were called to a disturbance. It's not a friendly place."

"This is Fred, he is a resident of the tunnels and he's going to guide us."

The white cop held out a folder. "Deacon said to give you these. It's an age progression photo of the suspect based on a picture from his online school yearbook. It's aged fourteen years; hopefully it looks like he does today."

I took the photos from the folder and passed

them around. I held one to Fred and asked. "Does this man look familiar?"

He took the photo and studied it carefully. "He looks familiar, but I can't really say. In the tunnels, many men have beards and are a little dirty most of the time."

"I understand, he could look totally different. Okay, let's go." We all moved out of the lobby and to our cars. I had Fred in my car and asked him to guide me to his tunnel. It may not be Hall's hidey hole, but it was as good a place as any to start.

He directed me to an area that was fenced off and I could see the opening to the tunnel below. We parked and got out of the cars. Fred showed us an opening in the fence that folded back so we could get down to the tunnel.

Fred led the way followed by me, Earl, Buck and the two giant cops taking up the rear. We went down the slight incline and up to the opening. We stopped at the opening as I turned to Fred.

"How far into the tunnel before we run into people?" I asked Fred.

"Not far, this is my tunnel, I live in one of the offshoot tunnels with about five other people. Well, three and a couple."

"Couple? Male and Female?"

"Yep, they're married. Lost their home and everything. The government forced them to live away from the normal. They are nice people, just want to be left alone now. They can't leave the country to get away from the crap the government dishes out. So they hide away from them. No name, no address, they disappear."

"Sounds like a way to vanish out of the system," I said.

Fred said, "That's exactly what they are doing."

*

Chapter 12

"Well, I'm happy for them. Now shall we go into the gates of hell?" I looked to everyone and smiled.

The big black cop, who I found out was called Eldridge, and didn't like being called El, said, "You lead the way, I've been in those tunnels before and it's not nice."

The white cop, called Smitty, said, "You can watch my back then."

"Oh, hell, no. We watch each other's backs." Eldridge said.

I looked to Fred, "Well, it's your home, you lead the way."

Fred, still holding his dog, smiled and moved towards the opening. "The smell isn't the best, so breathe through your mouths."

Earl said, "That's what they taught us when we go to a homicide that has a decomposed body. It works if you remember not to smell with your nose."

I looked to Buck and asked, "Did you get the lanterns?"

He looked at me and said, "Do you see any lanterns?"

I grimaced and went back to the car. I pulled out the high power lanterns I put in the back seat. Buck was behind me. "Sorry, I forgot to tell you to get them."

"Memory loss is a terrible thing at your age," he said with a big grin.

"I don't even want to hear it." I handed him two lamps and kept one for me, "Give the other to Earl."

We went back to the group. The cops had their high power flashlights out already and we proceeded into the opening of the tunnel.

I was feeling a little nervous, I'm not fond of confined spaces and the tunnel looked confining. It was basically a square tube and closed on four sides except the opening here at the entrance and probably at the other end, which wasn't visible for many miles ahead through the black hole in front of us. I felt like I was going to enter the jaws of death, or run into the devil. Fred was ahead of us and he had a small pocket flashlight that he brought out to help him get to his nest. I thought on that. It was funny to think, but it was like a nest. Like a rat would make in a small space.

"How far are you in here?" I asked him.

"Not far, I don't like being too far away from an exit, in case of trouble."

"Trouble?" Buck asked.

Fred looked back at him in the light of Buck's lantern. "Yep, floods, fights, wild dogs, whatever."

"Wild dogs?" Earl asked.

"Feral dogs, looking for food. No hell hounds, but close. They smell food and are hungry enough to take it. They have sharp teeth. I have to keep my food closed up."

"Wonderful," Eldridge said. "They didn't explain that to us the last time I was in these tunnels."

We came upon a man looking annoyed at intruders. "Who are you?" he challenged, holding a long lead pipe.

"Henry, relax. It's Fred."

"Oh, sorry Fred, I only saw those huge men behind you. What are they doing here?" he asked, then said, "They're cops, Fred. You bought cops."

"They're looking for a killer, Henry. Just relax, they won't bother you. May we pass through your place?"

"You are always welcome to enter. Since these people are your friends, I'll yield." He stepped out of the middle of the tunnel and over to a wall.

As we walked through led by Fred, I could see crates set up like shelves with various objects on them along with two candles. There was a makeshift bed on the ground with blankets and a pillow. Next to all his belongings was a shopping cart, empty. I figured he'd pack it if he had to evacuate due to a flood. I was stunned that people lived like this. We went further into the tunnel and found a couple more people camped out on the cement floor. Fred introduced us to the married couple. We didn't want to bother them, so we went on.

Fred finally pointed to a side tunnel and said, "I'm down there." He headed into the tunnel and we followed. He had quite a set up. Crate shelves and a nice bed with mattresses. There was a cabinet next to the bed and he went to unlock the combination lock sealing the cabinet. He opened it and pulled out a nice camp lantern. It had a crank on the side that he could turn to generate power to recharge the internal batteries. I had one like it years ago.

He flipped a switch and it lit up the area. The cops walked past his space and into the tunnel a ways. Buck and Earl waited with me by Fred.

"Have you ever thought about staying at one of the shelters in town?" I asked.

"They don't like it if you stay very long, and sometimes the shelters can be dangerous, too. It's a roof over people's heads, but their property is not always secured, and other shelter residents will rob people there, even beat them up after lights out. Plus many of the homeless shelters make everyone leave the building for the day and won't let anyone back in until like 5 or 6 at night. Some of them even make people leave as early as 6am. When you go out for the day, you have to take all of your belongings with you. Here I have everything I want and privacy, unless someone does come through."

We heard a voice at the end of the tunnel from where we came. "Hey Freddy, are you down there? You got your protection money?" The voice said as it came closer. Buck and Earl were standing just outside of the lighted area, so they couldn't be seen easily. The man who spoke came closer to where I could shine my light at him.

"Hey, get that the hell out of my eyes," he yelled. I moved it away, as he was blinking, probably blinded by the light.

"Damn, man I can't see now. What the hell is going on here? Who's this old man, Fred? You aren't inviting more people in, are you Fred?"

I stepped forward and said, "Who do you think you are?"

The man was greasy looking in the dim light of Fred's lamp. He blinked a couple more times and said, "What the hell do you care? Are you going to pay me, too?"

"For what?" I said.

"If you are going to stay here in this tunnel, you'll need to pay me for rent."

"Rent? I thought these tunnels were owned by Clark County. How is it you own them?"

"Because I say so." He growled.

"I don't think so," Buck growled back, stepping into the light where he could be seen. The greasy man looked surprised and his eyes went wide. Buck moved up to him and grabbed him by the front of his shirt. The man struggled, but you don't fight with Buck. He lifted the man off the ground and turned him towards Earl, who was coming forward now.

"Hey, Earl, shall we make a wish? You take one leg, I'll take the other."

Even in the dim light of Fred's lamp, I could see the greasy man was wetting his pants. Earl came close and wrinkled his nose. "He stinks, I'm not touching him. You can rip him apart yourself."

I was trying not to laugh when I heard movement behind me and the cops came back from out of the tunnel behind us. Smitty went up to Buck and asked, "Whachya got there?"

"A nasty piece of work trying to hit up Fred for protection money." Buck replied and gave the greasy man a shake.

Eldridge came up, scoped out the greasy man

and said, "Well, well, look what we got here. Jackie Gorchek. Hey, Jackie, you know there's an arrest warrant out for you?"

Jackie was having trouble talking because Buck was holding on to his throat now. Buck said, "Well, in that case, I'll turn this ball of slime over to you."

Eldridge smiled and said, "Thank ye kindly. Smitty, we need to get this man to lock-up before he has a terrible accident in these tunnels. He may fall down and hurt his self."

Eldridge took hold of Jackie and he nearly carried him back out the way we came in. Even in the dim light, I could see the terror in the greasy man's face. I smiled.

*

Chapter 13

"Hopefully he won't bother you again." I said. "I've heard of businesses paying protection money to the mob or gangs, but didn't think it could happen down here."

"Jackie is an ass, but he does some good. Keeps the riff-raff from bothering us." Fred said. "We sometimes get punk kids causing problems for us. Jackie has a gun and will use it if need be."

I was glad he hadn't pulled his gun on me. We heard two gunshots echoing through the tunnels. "Maybe Jackie pulled his gun on the cops?" I said.

Earl moved forward and said, "I'll go see if they need any help." He went back through the darkness. I could see his lamp bobbing in the gloom.

I wondered what justice was done to the greasy man. I turned back to Fred. "Okay, I need you to look at the picture again and try to remember if you've seen this man."

I handed him the photo sketch and he studied it. He shook his head slowly and said, "Like I said, he looks familiar, but I don't know if I've ever come across him, sorry."

Trick or Treat Murders

The dog was wiggling in Fred's arms. "Probably needs to take a crap," Fred said. He went to his cabinet and pulled out a length of rope and tied it to the dog's neck. He let the dog run out a ways, then the dog took a dump.

"Speaking of that, where's your toilet?" Buck asked.

"There's a smaller off shoot tunnel up ahead, everyone uses it for that. When it does flood from the rains, the tunnel gets cleaned out."

"Delightful," Buck said, scrunching his face.

"Fred, what did you do before you started living here?" I asked.

He looked like he was trying to remember. "I worked in a casino as a cash counter in the money rooms. That was one of the last casinos owned by the mobs. When the Feds finally convinced them to move on, I lost my job. The fancy corporation who bought out the casino didn't want mob employees still working there. Guess they figured we would steal from them. I was out of work and couldn't find another casino that would hire me. I just drifted after I lost everything. I had no money. I met a homeless man on a street and he taught me to survive. Then I found out about the tunnels. I guess I'm okay here."

I wasn't happy with this. The man was decent

and it seemed like life just crapped on him. "If you could, would you get out of the tunnels?"

He looked around and didn't say anything. Then he asked me, "Would you live here?"

That answered my question. "I can't help everyone, but I'm going to get you out of here, Fred. Gather anything that's important to you and we'll leave."

Fred looked apprehensive. "I don't know, this has been my home for all these years. I don't know if I could survive out there."

"Don't worry, I'll see to it you'll survive, now we'll help you to carry anything you need."

Fred slowly went to the cabinet and pulled out a box. He handed it to me and said, "That's the only important thing I'll need. I'll give the rest of this to Henry."

Fred picked up the dog and we walked back to the exit. When we came to Henry, Fred explained that he could have his space. Henry seemed pleased. "I'll stop and visit with you when I can, Henry." Fred said.

Henry smiled and started to gather his things for the move. We went back to the opening to go out and saw Earl standing with the cops up on the road. There was an EMS unit parked by them and they were just putting a gurney into the back. It drove out followed by the cops. We came up the embankment and Earl walked over to us.

"The fool thought he could escape and pulled a weapon. Luckily for him, Eldridge and Smitty only wounded him. They're taking him to LV Medical. He's not in good shape, but he's lucky to be alive."

"He can bleed out for all I care," Buck said. "Not nice what he was doing to all these poor people."

"So, anything on Hall?" Earl said.

"No, I hoped taking Fred back to the tunnel would help jog his memory." I said. "But he couldn't remember him. Hall could be looking different from this photo. It's only a supposed age progression."

"I'm not about to go digging through 500 miles of tunnels to find him. Our best bet is to wait for Halloween and catch him attempting to kill Lowbrill." Earl said.

"I guess that's the best situation." I said. "Well, we need to get back to the building and I need to get Fred into a new life."

Fred cracked a toothy smile and we all got back into the car. On the way back to the office, Buck looked back to Fred. "What are you going to name your puppy?" he asked.

Fred thought on it for a moment and said, "I don't know yet. A name will come to me and it will be a good name."

We rode the rest of the way in silence. I turned on the radio and found a station playing what sounded like classical music. I wasn't crazy about classical music, but it was soothing. I could see Earl was still following behind us in his car.

We arrived and I saw an unmarked police car in the parking lot. I presumed that Deacon was here. We went in the back door and I asked Buck to take Fred to the lounge and make him comfortable. Earl came in and I told him to follow me. I went up to the front and found Deacon standing at the counter talking to Lynn and Lacey.

"What do we owe the pleasure of this visit?" I asked.

"I was just out to the Lowbrill's residence and thought I'd swing by to see my favorite people. Find anything in the tunnels?"

"No. It's disgusting down there. I could never live like that."

"We have to deal with the homeless every day. Many of them camp out in alleys and on the street.

Trick or Treat Murders

We take a number of them to a couple shelters but they never stay."

Lynn said, "I once knew a man who worked with the homeless. He said most have mental problems and the hospitals won't deal with them because they can't pay for treatment. So they turn them loose on the city. To make matters worse, whole families are becoming homeless when they can't afford to pay their mortgages and are evicted. Most live out of their cars. It's good that it doesn't freeze here very often at night."

"What are you going to do with Fred?" Lacey asked.

"I'll see what options there are to get him a place to stay. Penny and I donate a good deal of money to the agencies that run the shelters, time to call in a marker or two."

"Good luck, there are a whole lot of homeless people struggling for shelter. Most of the soup kitchens are running at capacity to feed all these people, too." Deacon said.

"Well, I can always put him in my guesthouse," I said with a grin.

Lacey laughed and said, "Sure, and when Penny finds out, you'll be Fred's roommate."
*

Chapter 14

"Only until I can find him a place to stay," I defended myself.

"Good luck on that," Lacey said, and went back to her desk.

Lynn turned to me and said, "You know Jim, this place could be a shelter for him. The store room where Buck had his office is still partitioned, you could put a cot for him in there and the building has a bathroom and a shower. There's the fridge and microwave in the lounge and he could play pinball to keep occupied. He'd be our building security at night and on weekends."

"I could have him clean the building instead of having to pay the cleaning people to come in and do it. That would give him extra cash to spend. Not a bad idea, Lynn. I knew when we took you on, you'd be an asset." I said with a grin. "I'll have Buck help me set him up."

Earl said he was going to run some errands and said he'd see me bright and early the next morning.

Trick or Treat Murders

"Just don't call me before 8 AM," I said. He laughed, then left.

I excused myself and went to the lounge and found Buck and Fred playing foosball. Fred was winning. They stopped as I stood watching.

"What's on your mind, chief?" Buck asked.

I explained the idea to them and Fred loved it. "Fred, follow me and I'll show you where we can set you up." We went out of the room through the back door to the hallway in the back. Fred had his dog on the rope from the tunnel and the dog followed behind him. I led Fred and Buck to the storeroom where Buck previously had his office.

"Fred, this room has a partition that was used for an office. You can set up in here, we'll get you a small bed and shelves. There's a shower in the guard's room and you can put food in the fridge and cook it in the microwave."

"This would be a lot better than the tunnels," Buck said.

"Now, you'd have to work here, cleaning the building. Vacuuming and throwing out trash. I'll list your duties. I'm paying a cleaning crew now, but I'll pay you for what they're getting and cancel their services. That way you'd have some income."

"And there's TV in the lounge you can watch," Buck added.

Fred looked a little weepy. I didn't want to embarrass him so I told Buck to take him out and buy him some new clothes. I gave Buck the company credit card and said not to run it out.

"Come on Freddy, we're going shopping." Buck said.

I stopped Buck on their way out and said, "Get him some things for washing up, towels, soap, shampoo and some foods to start. If you can find a nice futon bed, pick one up. Take the van."

"You got it, I'll fix him up real nice." He went out, taking Fred to the van in the back parking area.

I went up front, Deacon and Lynn were still talking. "So what is the plan for protecting Lowbrill?" I asked Deacon.

"Well, the next two nights I've got men in the house and watching from outside. He's never struck on Devil's Night, but we will be watching."

"Is there a Mr. Lowbrill?"

"Nope, he passed away two years ago. Mrs. Lowbrill was really upset when she heard Jeffrey was murdered. She does have a daughter who lives in Reno."

"Well, at least she's not totally alone." I said. "I'm going into the restroom to wash the smell off myself the best I can. The tunnels are not the most sanitary place. I hope we have enough hand sanitizer left." I excused myself and went to the back. I figured on waiting around for Buck and Fred to return so I could help get him set up. I ran water on a hand towel and wiped my face and then squirted the sanitizer liberally on my hands.

I finished and went to my office and took out a piece of paper and wrote all the things Fred would need to do at night. It was getting late, but I stayed until they returned.

Fred looked like a little kid at Christmas when they came in with a number of packages. Buck said he got a futon and I went out to the van to help bring it in. We unpacked the big box and took all the parts out, laying them on the floor. We worked on it a short while before I stood, stretching my back. Buck said he'd stay around until he got the futon put together if I wanted to leave.

I was wearing down, so I took the offer. I knew Buck would keep Fred entertained. Since Buck had split with Maria he didn't have to go home, so I figured he'd be here late. I handed the list to Buck and said to fill Fred in on his duties. He said he'd take care of it.

I went back to the front and Deacon was gone. Lynn was getting ready to go. "How's your border doing?" she asked.

"So far, so good, help keep an eye on him until he gets used to us."

"Yes, we are an acquired taste. I think he'll be alright. Well, I'm going to go pick up the baby and then head home. See you in the morning." She went out the front door and was gone. Lacey was at the counter and I turned to her.

"Why don't you go get Tracey and head home, too. It's close enough to quitting time."

She smiled and picked up her purse and said, "See ya." She zipped out to the outer lobby where I could see her talking to Tracey. I never really understood why we needed Tracey out there, but she was a sweet girl who needed the work. They both went out the front door and it was now quiet in the place.

I could hear Buck banging around with the futon. I locked up the front doors and thought about getting a key for Fred out of my desk drawer. I got the key and went back to the store room and told Buck I was leaving. He waved me off as he and Fred kept working on the futon. I gave the key to Fred.

Trick or Treat Murders

I was heading to the back door when I heard my name. "Mr. Richards, I just want to thank you so much for this. I guess finding your little dog was a gift from Heaven."

"I'm happy to help. You'll do fine." I turned to the door and went out to my Crown Vic.

I drove to the house wondering what Penny was up to. I pulled into the drive and parked the car in the garage. I went in the house and found Penny and Willy both on the couch, sound asleep. I kissed Penny on the forehead and went to my home office.

I sat at my computer and started it up. I figured on writing some more of my latest book, but I sat there not feeling it. Sometimes I don't have the inspiration to write, so I opened up a browser and explored all I could find on Google about the homeless in Las Vegas. I couldn't believe how many topics there were.

*

Chapter 15

I was reading the statistics about the number of homeless in Vegas and said quietly to myself, "There's one less homeless person today."

"What did you say sweetie?" Came a voice from at my door. It was Penny, still looking sleepy.

"I was just exploring the web about the homeless in Las Vegas. I can't believe what goes on here to try and help these people. But it seems they aren't getting through to enough of them."

"A lot of them don't want to be helped. It's a sad fact." Penny came over to the chair next to my desk and sat. "A lot of them have mental problems that need treatment, but they don't get it. Speaking about homeless, what did you do with Fred?"

I smiled and said, "I put him in our guesthouse."

She just stared at me. I was ready for her to hit me, but she didn't. I laughed and said, "No, I didn't. Lynn made a good suggestion today about what to do with him." I explained the set up and about putting him in the store room. Then I covered having Buck take him shopping. That's when she hit me.

"Hey, what's that for?" I asked.

"For not asking me to take him shopping. I'll just have to take him tomorrow for more clothes. One can never have enough clothes."

"It's what you always say. That's your motto." She didn't hit me again.

"So, Fred is now the live-in custodial and night watchman?"

"I guess you could say that. He's a nice guy who had a bad break in life. I hope this gets him back on his feet."

"You are just the conquering hero aren't you?"

"I'm not trying to be a hero, I'm just troubled by injustice to humans. Although I prefer animals."

"I'm your favorite animal, aren't I?"

"Yep, wild cat and squirrel monkey." I laughed and she hit me.

The next morning, I arrived at work earlier than usual. Nobody was in yet and I wanted to see if Fred was all right. I entered the front door this time. The room looked clean, the waiting area was straight and looked vacuumed. Then I saw the flowers on the counter. I went to them and saw they were fresh. I turned to see Fred coming in through the glass doors from the back. He gave me a grin.

"Nice flowers, Fred. Did you put them here?"

"I did. I took an early morning walk over to Tropicana Road to where there was a store selling flowers out front. So, I got some for Miss Lacey, Miss Tracey and I put some in Miss Lynn's office, too."

"I hope you didn't put any in the men's offices." He laughed and I said, "I haven't paid you yet, I'm sorry. I'll fix that. How did you pay for the flowers?"

"I had some savings in my box I brought from the tunnel. They didn't cost much. The vases were in the store room, so I put the flowers in them."

"Well, I'm sure Lacey, Tracey and Lynn will appreciate the gesture. Did you have a good night?"

"Yes, sir, I did. Slept very well. Nice to not hear people complaining or crying."

"My name is Jim, so please use it. Sir is for old

men and royalty, I'm not either."

"Sorry, force of habit. My mother taught me well."

"Okay," I said and took money out of my pocket. "Here's your first week's wages so you don't have to use your savings. I'm sorry I didn't give this to you last night. I didn't think about you having to go out."

"Well, I did a lot of roaming around the city while I lived in the tunnels. I did that to get away from being there."

"There are a lot of people living on the streets, but you chose the tunnels?"

"On the streets, there are bad people that can bother you. And some people don't like homeless on their property. In the tunnel, they leave you alone. Oh, Mr. Earl is in his office. He came in early."

"Thank you, Fred. Just enjoy your day whatever you want to do."

"Who takes care of the lawn and the flowers outside?"

I had to think. "There is some landscaping company who comes in to cut the grass, the flowers just grow. I don't know who tends to them, flower fairies I guess."

"I can take care of that if you have a mower. I love to work with plants. I missed that being homeless."

"Okay Fred, you have a new duty and an increase in your salary. I'll have Buck run over to get a mower. You can go along to help him."

"Great." He smiled and I excused myself. I went back to my office and put my briefcase down, then went to Earl's office.

"What up, doc?" I said coming into the room.

He grinned and said, "I was thinking about the costume the kid wore when he murdered his mother. I figured he would wear it again so I called Deacon and he got me street surveillance video of the second murder, the next year. I've been going through it and found the little bugger heading to the woman's house. Same costume, a bag over the head, plaid shirt and jeans. I figured if he was living in the tunnels, he wouldn't have a big selection of costumes."

"Good deducing, Mr. Chan."

He gave me a look. I said, "Charlie Chan, the detective from the old movies."

He shook his head and said, "You old people and your silent movies."

105

"Hey, those movies had sound and I'm not that old. I watch the classic movies on TV."

"Whatever, now you can watch this movie from thirteen years ago."

"I'm surprised the city kept the video that long."

"It was police property, the city erases them after a couple weeks. That's why having Deacon around comes in handy."

He reached to the mouse and clicked the video player. "This is the part that the police copied out from the surveillance video." The video started and I leaned forward.

The quality wasn't the best, but we could see the boy walking down the street and turning onto the sidewalk of the second victim's home. We couldn't see the porch very well, there was a tree in front, but the leaves were sparse, so we could barely see him at the door. The woman answered and they talked briefly, then he shot her. He calmly walked away and back down the street.

"He went the same direction he came from, so he was probably going back to his hideout," I said.

"Deacon said they checked the cameras on the streets and they followed him the best they could, but he went to an area where they don't have cameras." He stood and told me to follow him.

We went into my office and he went to the map still on the wall. He pointed to where the house was for the second murder. "The woman was murdered here. Now, the cameras caught him going in this direction, if I figured correctly." He was guiding the path with his finger until he said, "This is where the cameras end," and pointed to the last place Hall was seen.

I moved closer to the map and studied it. Then I saw it. "Look here, there is a flood canal along that road, and it leads to a tunnel here," I said pointing. "His front door, I'd say."

*

Chapter 16

"I'm not about to go back into the tunnels. But, we know where he is possibly going. I'm just wondering why he's doing this. I think we need to get into his mind, maybe head him off that way." Earl said.

"What do you propose?"

"Don't say propose. It's not a word I like. I'm figuring that if we can get a few of the boys from his class together, we can find out why he's killing their mothers."

"I can see that. You have the list from the school; does it have any phone numbers?" I asked.

Earl pulled the list from his jacket pocket and looked. "There are next of kin numbers here, I'll call around and see if we can get them together."

"Maybe a long shot, but if Hall is striking out at their moms, they must know why. Go ahead and have them come here, we can talk in the conference room."

"I'm on it," he said and left the room.

I heard the back door close and went out to see if it was Buck. It was. He went to the door to the addition where his office was and I followed.

"Hey buddy," I said as I entered his office, "I need you to do a favor."

"Speak, oh great one," he said with a grin.

"Take Fred and go get a lawn mower. Nothing big, just a small riding mower. I know you'll want to get the biggest and fastest one they have, but don't, please."

Buck laughed and said, "I can get a decent one. Thinking of having Fred do the lawn?"

"He offered, so he has the job."

"I'll go round him up and we'll be back. Where should I put the thing?"

I had to think on that. "See if you can get one of those small sheds that you assemble and put it behind the building."

"Sounds like a winner." Buck went out, followed by me. I went to the front to see if Lacey was in yet. I went through the addition's door to the front and Lacey was at the counter admiring the flowers.

Trick or Treat Murders

She turned and saw me. "Did you do this?"

"Fred did. He went out early this morning and got them. One for you, Tracey and Lynn."

"That is so sweet. I like him more, now," Lacey said as she smelled the flowers.

The door from the outer lobby opened and Tracey came in, "Jim, there's a man out here who wants to talk to a detective."

"We have private investigators, but no detectives. He can see the police for that."

"Well, he is the police," she said.

"Oh, well, send him in."

She went back to the outer lobby. Shortly, a man came in and asked, "Is this where I find Jim Richards and his detectives?"

"I'm Jim Richards, we have only private investigators, no detectives, what can I do for you?"

"I'm Deputy Les Amico, LA County Sheriff's Department, and I was referred to this office. I have a small problem and could use your help."

"Well, follow me to my office and I'll see what we can do." I led him to my office and asked him to sit. "Now, what can I do for you?"

He seemed hesitant, then said, "My daughter is missing and I found out she's in Vegas. I don't know where, but I have no jurisdiction here, and I don't want to involve the Vegas police."

"Why do you think she's here?"

"One of her friends told me. She got involved with some photographer who said he'd bring her here for a photo shoot for some Vegas advertising company. I got his name, but wasn't able to find any info on the man, and there is no company for that advertising agency. I need help finding her. I think she may be in danger."

"Why don't you want to involve the police? This sounds like something they should be handling."

He was hesitant again. "My daughter is troubled. She has a conviction on her record and I don't want her involved with any criminal activity, she would be violating her parole and would go back to jail. I went to a lot of trouble to get her out. She also wasn't supposed to leave LA County as terms of her parole." He paused again, I could see he was in distress.

"So you want us to extract her so you can take her back. What if she doesn't want to go?"

"If it comes down to that, I guess I'd have to get

111

the police on it and she'd be taken back forcibly. I don't want to see her go back to jail, but I can't have her getting deeper into crime."

"Other than parole violation, she hasn't committed any crime so far. I'm on a case to find a killer who may strike again on Halloween, but I'll have you talk to one of our investigators to see if she can help you."

"She?"

"Yes, Lynn DeAngelo, former LVPD homicide Lieutenant. She retired and joined my firm. She's real good at her job. I know, I've worked with her. She knows a lot about Vegas and the crime scene here. I'll see if she's in yet and have her talk to you." I stood and said I'd return.

I went back to the front and asked Lacey if Lynn was in.

"Yes, she just went into her office."

"Thanks," I said and went there. She was at her desk sorting papers.

"Jim, what's up," she said as I entered. "Where did the flowers come from?"

"Fred got them this morning. I've got a distressed father in my office looking for his daughter." I briefly explained and asked, "Can you take it?"

"Let me talk to him. He's an LA County Sheriff? You know they are the largest Sheriff's Department in the world. They have more than 18,000 employees; over 9,100 are sworn deputies, with over 8,000 civilians, and an additional 4,200 civilian volunteers, and 900 reserve Deputies."

"Well, aren't you just a Wikipedia of information," I said.

"I was thinking of transferring to them just before I met Deacon. I had to know about them before I went charging in."

"Then you'll have something to talk about with Amico. I'll bring him to you." She thanked me and I went out.

I got Amico settled in with Lynn and went back to see Earl. He was on the phone. I sat in his client chair. He finished and smiled.

"I got hold of ten of the sons, two are out of the country, and the remaining eight are interested in finding out what happened to their mothers. I have them coming in at two this afternoon."

"Good. We'll hit them up with the news that Tony Hall is still alive. You know, I was thinking that maybe if Hall kills off all the women, he may go after his classmates. He's already murdered Jeffrey."

"If he's turned serial killer, I wouldn't put it past him to do so. Something to mention to the boys."

"They aren't boys now, they are all over 28, so they're adults. I think I'll call Deacon and have him join us."

"Did someone mention my name?" Deacon asked as he entered.

"You know, you've been doing a lot of that lately." I said. "Are you standing outside our doors waiting for us to mention your name?"

He just grinned and sat.

*

Chapter 17

"So what's the scoop?" Deacon asked.

"We're having Hall's former classmates come in to have a talk to see if we can figure out what's pushing Hall into committing murder." I said. "We figure they may know Hall better than anyone."

"I like it. The investigating officers who caught the cases over the years never associated the students. First, they figured Hall was dead, so why bother to connect the classmates. They never thought to exhume the body to see if he was in there. They were looking to connect the women." Deacon said. "They went in the wrong direction. They didn't know the women were connected by their sons."

"We don't know Hall's mental state, but he has the M.O. of a serial killer, a very patient serial killer. But nevertheless, this is methodical and aimed at a specific group of people. Mothers." I said.

"Hopefully his classmates will shine some light on him." Earl said. "They knew him back then, and they are the only ones we know of who did. Can't ask his mother, and his father is not functioning on all cylinders. I suppose you'd care to join us?"

"Hell, yeah. I need to know what's going on so I can keep Weber happy." He laughed. "How's Fred doing?"

"Great, he's working out real good. He and Buck went out to get a lawnmower. Fred is now our gardener and landscaping person, and he agreed to all this on his own."

"I'm glad to see one homeless person get out of the gutter. Too bad this country spends more on defense and foreign countries than helping our own people." Deacon said.

"Don't start me on the bad habits of our country." I said, when I heard the back door close. "Excuse me, I think Buck has returned." I went out to the hallway and saw Buck and Fred going into the storeroom. I followed.

Buck was getting our big tool box with all the power tools. He saw me and grinned. "Got a nice shed, but we have to put it together. Fred and I will be busy out back working on it. This is fun. Oh, and we picked up a bunch of flowers and a couple trees to plant."

I stood out of the way. Fred had his dog on a nice new leash. I guess he bought one at the store. The three of them went back out the door. I turned to see Lynn coming down the hallway.

"So, how'd it go with Amico?" I asked.

"I'm going to help him. I know a few people in town that can help me track down this photographer. The advertising agency that was mentioned is non-existent. The guy lied to her, so I figure it was not for a modeling session. I hope this isn't going into human trafficking. But, I'll bet on it."

"Did Amico leave?"

"Yeah, he's staying at a motel up on Charleston. I have his cell phone number. He wants to come along when I go out. Since he's a cop, I agreed. I did warn him not to do anything to the photog if we find him."

"Good, keep me in the loop. I have a bunch of people coming in shortly about the Trick-or-Treat Killer."

"I hope you find him, Halloween is for haunting and frightening people, not for murder."

"I think all the slasher movies aren't exactly helping to keep our children mentally balanced." I said.

"I agree, my daughter is going to be monitored to teach her right from wrong, fake from fact."

Trick or Treat Murders

I smiled when I saw Deacon, who had walked up and stood silently behind Lynn. I looked at him and said, "For such a big man, you sure are quiet."

Lynn spun around and hit him. "I told you to not sneak up on me."

He laughed and kissed her.

"I have a case to go investigate, so I'll see you later," she said and went off.

"So, where are you going to question the eight men?" Deacon asked.

I said, "In our conference room. Help me get it set up." I turned and went down the hall to the room. Normally, Buck used the room for his guards to have meetings. The chairs were spread out around the room so I had Deacon help arrange them in a half circle so we could see the men better.

"Now to see what we can find out from the boys," I said and went back to Earl's office. Deacon followed.

"Do you want to lead in the questioning?" Earl asked.

"We can both take turns. Or we can divide them up, ask them about Hall and see if they have the same stories." I said.

Deacon said, "I find separating them works well. Play them against each other."

"You are the expert, and you can interrogate a couple yourself." I said.

"Be glad to." Deacon replied.

Lacey came to the door and said, "You have guests." Then turned and went off.

"Who hired her?" Earl asked.

I held up my hand, and then stood. "Shall we go greet our guests?"

We went up front and found four men, all horse-playing with each other.

"Excuse me, gentlemen. Can you relax?" I said loudly so they could hear over their goofing around.

They stopped and turned to us. Deacon and Earl went around me to the counter. I stood in the middle of the men and said, "I'd like you to follow me, please."

They followed me to the room with Deacon and Earl following behind. I had them sit and asked them what they were doing.

Trick or Treat Murders

One man said, "We haven't seen each other in years. We were just fooling around."

"Okay, just behave and we'll be with you shortly. We're waiting for the rest of your friends. And don't attack them, please. This big man is a cop and he can arrest any of you for disorderly conduct."

They looked at Deacon, he grinned and pulled his jacket back to show his badge. They went quiet.

I went back out to the front and found four more men coming in, all babbling to each other. I knew we were going to have a tough time with them.

I took them to the room and it was pandemonium when they saw each other. Deacon used his cop voice and yelled, "Break it up!!"

They all stopped and looked at Deacon with a slight fear in their eyes. He had that effect.

"Gentlemen, be seated," I said.

They sat and went quiet. "Good, now we have to talk. These men are a cop and a private eye. I'm the head private eye here. So I will be conducting this session. Now, I need everyone to identify themselves." I pointed to the first man in the semi-circle.

"Uh, I'm Mark Downs."

I looked back to Earl, he checked off the name on his list.

"Next," I said.

"Ralph Reslen," he said.

Again, Earl checked him off.

I went down the row of friends and then came to the last. Earl was smiling and nodded.

"Okay, we need to talk to you about Anthony Hall." I waited to see what reaction I would get. Most of them looked shocked. I half expected that. But for them to go totally silent wasn't expected.

I looked at Deacon and Earl, then turned back to the men. "Well, this should be interesting."

*

Chapter 18

"Gentlemen, if you knew Anthony—or Tony—Hall, please raise your hand." I asked.

They all did.

"Good, then this will be easy. How many of you knew that Tony Hall died back when you were in school with him?"

Again, they all raised their hands.

"Good, now how many of you knew Tony wasn't really dead?"

Half of them started to raise their hands, then stopped and looked surprised.

I wanted to laugh at their sudden change in attention. They were all being so flippant together and having a good time, now they heard something that took the wind out of their sails.

One man, Ralph Reslen, said, "What the hell are you talking about. Tony was murdered. I went to his funeral."

"Well, we exhumed his body the other day and it turns out it's not him in the grave. Any of you know where he went?"

They all stared in stunned silence. "I'll take that as a no," I said.

"Okay, my associates and I would like to talk to you individually, so let's start with the three of you." I pointed to the first three. "The rest of you can just sit and wait."

I pulled my cell phone and called Buck out in the back and asked him to come back in to help me with something. He came in and I asked him to make sure none of the men left the room. He grinned and said it would be his pleasure.

Deacon took one man to Buck's security guard office, I took one to mine, and Earl took the third to his office.

I told the man with me to sit, and he did.

"Ralph, you mentioned in the other room that you attended Tony Hall's funeral. Were you and he close friends?"

The man paused for a moment and then said, "No, I just wanted to see a funeral. I snuck in and sat in the back, watching. It was closed casket, so I never got to see the body. I never cared for Tony, he was a little pain in the ass."

"How so?"

"Hard to explain. Haven't you ever had someone in your class that you just had to hate?"

I thought back to my class reunion a couple months back and a few people came to mind. "Yes, I think everyone knows someone like that. I don't like to bring up this subject, but your mother was murdered on Halloween."

He seemed to pale a little, looking disturbed. "It not something I like to remember, but yes, she was."

"The police never found out who did it, did they?"

"No, I can't imagine why she was even murdered. Why are you asking this and what does this have to do with Tony still being alive?"

"I don't know if you are aware that every Halloween for the last fourteen, a mother has been murdered, just like yours." He gave me a blank stare. "We think that Tony Hall is behind those murders. And the victims were all the mothers of your friends out there."

Now he sat up straight and said, "What the hell.

Why would Tony murder my mother, let alone all the others?"

"That's what we are trying to find out. Did Tony ever have a reason to hate you so much that he would kill your mother?"

Now he sat back and looked down at the floor. He didn't say anything, but looked like he was mulling something over in his head.

"Ralph, do you have something to tell me?" I asked.

He looked up to me and said, "He had a reason to hate all of us. Every guy in our class didn't like him. We all ganged up on him one day at recess and took him into the gym." He had a look on his face that told me they did something bad. "We hung him upside down from one of the climbing ropes, and left him there. They said he passed out from the blood running to his head from being up there so long. They had to take him to the hospital."

"Okay, he definitely had something to hate all of you. But why kill your mothers?"

He looked to me again, not smiling. "We heard, just after the incident, that he was an abused kid. His mother would take everything out on him. He even lost his shoes to Jeff Lowbrill because his mother accused him of stealing them. I heard he got a good beating for that. Maybe he hated mothers?"

"You mentioned Jeff Lowbrill, did you know that Jeff was murdered the other day?"

Now Ralph looked panicky, "Is Tony murdering us now?"

"We don't know. That's why we are asking all of you to help." I sat back and continued, "I have enough for now. Just be alert for anything. Tony may have murdered the mothers, but he did only one a year on Halloween. We believe his own mother was his first kill and has gone after each of your mothers every year since then. There is one more mother left of your group, and we are going to protect her."

I stood and said he could go. I asked him to go up front to the lobby waiting area and rest. I pointed the way and he left. I went to Earl's door and said to send his man to the lobby. Earl was standing and came over to me. I said I didn't want these men talking to the others before we spoke with them. He agreed.

Deacon was coming out of the guard office with his man. I told him the same I told Earl. The men went to the front as we went back to the conference room.

It was quiet in the room, a little conversation, but quiet. I asked Buck how they were doing out back.

126

"Fred is a real handy man. He's just about got the shed together. I expect it to be finished when I get back out there."

"Okay, go back out. Thanks for watching them." I said and he left.

The three of us went back into the room. The men looked at us and waited.

"So, you all did Tony a bad deed? Did you think of the consequences of what you did?" I asked.

One man spoke up, "We didn't think it would result in him faking his death."

"You think he faked it? Why?"

"We were talking and decided if he's still alive, then he had to have faked his death. Mostly to get away from his mother. We all heard, after he supposedly died, that his mother had been a real abuser. Used to beat him something fierce. We felt bad for treating him like we did. Also, while we talked, it came out that all our mothers were murdered. Did Tony do this because of the way we treated him? Getting back at us through our mothers to make us hurt?"

"I'm starting to think that. We have one mother left out of your group. Jeff Lowbrill's mother. I don't suppose any of you know that Jeff was murdered the other day?"

They all looked stunned. "Did Tony do it?" asked one man.

"It looks that way. The same gun used in all the Halloween murders was used on Jeff. It has to be Tony."

"If Tony is running out of moms to kill, will he come after us?" another asked.

"If I were all of you, I'd watch your backs."

*

Chapter 19

You could hear a spider walking up the wall, it was so quiet.

"What do we do?" One man finally asked.

"I'd say just watch for anything out of the ordinary. We have plans for catching Tony on Halloween, so hopefully this will be finished. I think we have enough for now and you have been informed of the situation, so go and be careful."

They stood and left.

"Didn't you want to talk to the rest of them?" Earl asked after the room cleared.

"I'd say if you and Deacon compare notes with me you'll find they are all the same. Which what the rest of the men would say. I think we got enough to know what Tony is about. I'd like to talk to Hall's father." I looked to Earl, "Can you get him to come in?"

"I can, even if I have to drag him."

Trick or Treat Murders

"Hopefully not. Just convince him to come in." I turned to Deacon and said, "Anything on the Lowbrill woman?"

"She's not happy to be confined to her home, but she also doesn't want to die. So, she's good with hanging out until after Halloween."

Earl asked, "Do you think the sons should have some protection?"

"My guy said that there was always someone you didn't like in school, I'd say for me, it would be all those men. Let them watch out for themselves." I said.

Buck and Fred came in the conference room. "Want to see the masterpiece out back?" Buck said with a grin.

We all followed them outside and saw the shed standing tall on the back corner of the building. Buck opened the doors and we could see a nice riding lawnmower inside.

"Very good, guys." I turned to Fred and said, "Don't you leave us now, or I'll end up having to cut the grass by myself."

"Don't worry, I won't go anywhere," he replied with a big smile.

~~*~~

Lynn had Amico in her car as they drove up to an apartment on the north end of the strip.

"I don't mind you tagging along, just don't go commando when we find the creep," Lynn said.

Amico sat quietly, which worried Lynn.

They arrived at the apartment building and went to a door that Lynn had visited before. She knocked and waited. A few minutes later, the door opened and a young black girl stood staring at Lynn.

"Whatcha all want now, Lieutenant?" she said.

"Mabel, you'll be happy to know I'm not a cop anymore. So you have nothing to worry about. I just need information."

The girl looked a little more at ease. "Info costs ya," she said.

"Have you forgotten about the last time you got busted in that murder case I pulled? I helped you skate on the pandering charges. You owe me one."

The girl thought on that, then she eyed Amico. "Who that?" she asked.

131

Trick or Treat Murders

"This man is a deputy with the LA Sheriff's Department, he's looking for someone and I'm helping him. Now, I need to know where Louie Fine is making his crib."

"Louie? I ain't seen Louie in a month, at least."

"Where was he last? Where was he doing his photo shoots?"

"Some dive-ass building up in North Vegas by the Food for Less. I'll get ya the address." She went back into the darkness of the apartment. Lynn could see into her living area and saw the drug paraphernalia on a coffee table. Lynn wasn't a cop anymore and she had better things to do than hassle the girl right now.

She came back with a worn-out card for Louie Fine Photography. "Here, it be the last place I knew he was at. Don'tcha go telling him where y'all got it, ya hear?"

"Thanks Mabel, we're square now. Stay out of trouble and hide all the drug stuff on your table. Too easy to see from the door, probable cause and all that."

Mabel looked back and smiled. "Thanks ex-cop girl." She closed the door.

Amico said, "Aren't you going to turn her in?"

"Despite the fact she's a hooker and a junkie, she's a CI for a number of cops."

"Being an informant shouldn't excuse her from arrest."

"Look, do you want me to waste time with paperwork while they book her, or go find your daughter?"

He shut up and Lynn said, "I thought so." She went back to her car followed by the man.

They drove up to North Vegas and parked out front of the building addressed on the card.

"If he's in here, let me handle him, you find your daughter. Understood?"

"Yeah, I got it," he grumbled.

Lynn tried to look through the windows of the building, but they were covered well with newspapers. "Let's check around back to see if there's a door we can bust in."

"What about a warrant?" Amico asked.

"Les, I'm not a cop. You'll have to stay back as I enter, since you are one. You can follow me in then."

Trick or Treat Murders

They found an old wooden door in the back next to a dumpster. Lynn pushed her hand against it to see how sturdy it was. The door was like the building, old and falling apart. She put her shoulder to the door and gave a shove. The door frame splintered and opened easily.

"I guess Louie doesn't worry about break-ins." She entered the building and had her weapon out. She told Amico to keep his holstered.

They went down a hallway and heard muffled voices. Lynn went up to a door and could hear the voices better now.

"Oh, you are going to be so pretty in this. Now, struggle a little more. The bondage freaks love this crap."

Lynn carefully opened the door and could see the man at his camera, but couldn't see who he was photographing. A partition was in the way. She quietly entered as the man had his back to her.

Amico lumbered in and yelled, "Where's my daughter you slimebag!"

He went around the partition and found his daughter bound to a wall, struggling on a dirty mattress, gagged by some leather looking device. She was trying to get out of the straps holding her down.

Louie was yelling, "What the hell is this!"

Lynn brought her Sig Sauer up to his face and said, "Shut up, we just need the girl."

Amico was tearing the bindings from the wall and took the gag from her mouth.

"Oh Dad, I'm so glad you found me," she cried tearfully. They hugged, then Amico let her loose and charged at Louie.

Lynn got in front of him and yelled into his face, "Stop Les! You said you wouldn't harm him. I'll take care of that." She gave the big man a shove back. "Go take care of your daughter!"

Amico stood staring at Louie, then turned back to his daughter. Lynn grabbed Louie by the shirt and pulled him over to the girl. "Did this man forcibly bring you here?"

The girl was crying and nodded her head. Lynn contemplated on how to handle the situation. If she brought in the cops, then the daughter would be part of the investigation. Amico didn't want her to be in the system here. Lynn pushed Louie down into a chair and told him not to move. She called to Amico and he came over.

"You have a decision to make," she said.

Chapter 20

"What do you mean let him go? He kidnapped my daughter!" Amico bellowed as he stared at Louie. "I want justice for this atrocity!"

"Yes, I understand and I agree, but you wanted this to be kept quiet so your daughter wouldn't be in violation of her parole." Lynn said.

"She'd only violate her parole if she willingly left LA County. She was kidnapped and forced to come here. That makes a difference," he replied.

Lynn had to think on that. He was right in a sense. "Okay, since this was kidnapping across state lines, I know a man in the FBI who can handle this, and keep the local cops out of it. How's that sound?"

Amico smiled and said, "Works for me."

Lynn pulled her cell phone and placed a call.

Earl had talked to Mr. Hall and convinced him come in to the office. They drove their individual cars and parked in the back parking lot. Earl was coming up to the building and found Fred and Buck putting plants and flowers in the area behind the building. There were flower flats all over the place and a couple small trees with roots wrapped in burlap bags.

"Buck, are you becoming our gardener also?" Earl asked.

"I like flowers and plants, too. Fred has some great ideas to beautify the back area." Buck replied. "I can see that the back needs some improvement. A nice garden of flowers and plants can make our days start better." Earl just grinned and took Hall into the building.

I was in my office when Earl brought Hall in. "Jim, here's Mr. Hall."

"Please, call me Alvin," he said.

"Okay, Alvin, have a seat." Earl pointed to my client chair as I stood and motioned him to the chair.

"Thank you for coming in, Alvin. I have some questions to ask you, if you don't mind?" I said.

"No, if it helps find my son, I'll be glad to answer any question you have," he said as he sat. Earl took a chair by the wall and sat.

"Al…may I call you Al?" I asked.

"Certainly," he replied.

"Thanks Al, I need to know something that may be personal, but we need to understand your son's mental state." I paused to let that sink in. "Could you tell me about your wife's relationship with your son?"

"What do you mean by relationship?"

"Well, did they get along. Were they on good terms, or did they fight? How was the home life with them?"

He sat staring at the wall behind me. He was quiet for a bit then said, "My wife and Tony got along fine. Tony was a good son, never caused any problems. At least not while I was around."

"Al, I have heard from a number of people who say that Tony was abused by his mother."

Hall gave me a concerned look, "My wife never abused Tony. They got along fine," he said defensibly. "Who would make such statements as that?"

138

"People who knew Tony. His school classmates, boys who knew him. They say he was treated badly by his mother. The shoe incident that you didn't know about, Tony's mother made him give a new pair of shoes to another boy because she accused Tony of stealing them. They belonged to Tony. Then from what we heard, she beat him over the incident."

Hall went silent and looked down at the floor. I didn't want to push him, this was a delicate point I was making. He finally spoke, "I bought those shoes for Tony. Nothing was said as to what happened to them. I didn't ask. My wife was a little overbearing. I usually just didn't get into her affairs with my son."

"Then you think she may have abused him?'

"I wasn't home a lot. My business kept me away more than I wanted. But it was good in a way. My wife and I never got along very well. She was a mean woman. Yes, I'm sure she abused Tony, I just never wanted to acknowledge it. I'm sorry."

"Don't apologize to me. Tony is the person you should apologize to." I said.

"I don't know if I want to even talk to him now. If he did murder all those women, he's dead to me still. I make no excuses for him. He was a troubled kid. He was rude and meaner than my wife most of the time. At least to me he was. I don't think he ever talked back to my wife. She frightened me most of the time and I'm sure Tony was afraid of her, too."

"Do you know if Tony ever killed any animals?"

Hall looked to me, "Why do you ask that?"

"We believe that your son is a serial killer and studies show most of them have killed animals when they were adolescents. Did Tony ever do that?"

He didn't speak, I waited. "I got him a cat when he was twelve, just before he was murdered, or not. Whatever. The cat disappeared a few days later. Tony said he had no idea where the cat went to. My wife yelled at me about my wanting to get him the cat. It was the same with a hamster we got him a year before the cat. It disappeared about a week after he got it. He said it got out of its cage."

"So we can assume that he possibly disposed of the animals."

"Killed them, yes. I think he may have," Hill said.

I sat back. I didn't want this man to suffer more than he already had. "Al, this is not something I wanted to say to make you upset. We just need to know what we are up against."

He sat quietly and then said, "My son is a
140

monster. That's what you're up against. He murdered his own mother and more women. I can't forgive him for that. If you find him, put him down." He stood and left my office.

I stared at Earl, that wasn't expected. Earl stood and came over to me.

"Jim, it had to be asked. We have to get under Tony Hall's skin and stop him. I have to feel for the man. He went through the death of his son and wife. Now he finds that his son is alive and most likely murdered his wife. Did you expect a happy ending?"

"I'm past the fact that a son can murder their parents. I've seen it and read about it too many times. Daughters, too. It doesn't make it any less horrible. I don't agree with Tony killing all these women, but he had a reason for lashing out. Abuse."

"Maybe we need another vigilante to take out the abusers."

I thought about the Vegas Vigilante who was murdering the men who abused their families. That's how we got Jessie. Frankly, I don't believe abusers deserve to live. It's horrible what they do. And it seems they get away with it, until something really awful happens.

I looked up at Earl and said, "Shall we start a new branch in our firm to rid the world of abusers?"

Earl smiled and said, "Jim, I agree, but I don't think Deacon would like having to arrest us."

*

Chapter 21

Lynn was standing in the lobby of the photographer's building. Louie evidently didn't like cleaning, so the place was a mess. FBI Agent Frank Droben was just entering with a couple agents.

"Hey, Frank, good to see you again." Lynn said as he came up.

"Lynn, it's always a pleasure when you call with some problem. Kidnaping, eh?" he said.

"Yeah, and possibly more. Come on in the back and I'll explain." She led the men to the studio where Louie was sitting being watched by Amico, who was still holding on to his daughter.

"Frank, this is Deputy Les Amico, LA County Sheriff's Department and the girl is his daughter.

She's the victim," Lynn said, then went to Louie. "This piece of crap is Louie Fine, supposed photographer who lures women into coming here, then makes bondage videos. Trouble is, they are really bound and also prisoners. Follow me."

Lynn took him to another room where they found four sets of chains attached to the walls with filthy, stained mattresses below each set. "I have a feeling Louie had more than one woman here. He may be involved with human trafficking, but that's for you to figure out. I've solved my case, and after you get a statement from Amico's daughter, I'll be on my way."

"I guess you've done me a service with this, Lynn. Thanks, and I owe you one."

They went back into the studio and Droben had his men take Louie out. He asked Amico if he could bring his daughter to the local FBI building to give a statement. Amico explained that he came with Lynn and his car was at his motel.

"No, problem. You two can come with me and I'll take you back to your motel," Droben said.

They all went out of the building to their cars, then Lynn stood watching them getting ready to leave. Amico told Lynn to send him a bill, but Lynn said it was too easy, to save his money. He thanked her and got in Agent Droben's car.

Trick or Treat Murders

They left and Lynn got into her car. She sat for a minute, feeling pretty good about how the events unfolded. She always felt that way when she would wrap up a case while she was on the Vegas police, but this felt better. She started the car and drove back to her office.

~~*~~

I was talking to Deacon on the speaker phone, explaining what we found out from the father. "We are down to Devil's Night and then Halloween. I'm sure you can catch him at Lowbrill's home. I think you got enough information on Hall to do your job. I also think I'm finished with this."

"Jim, I appreciate everything you've done on this case. I'm sure we can nab Hall now. I'll see you get a certificate of appreciation from the department." Deacon's voice came out of the speaker.

"Certificate? I want remuneration. You know, cash. I can't pay the bills with certificates."

"Jim, you are so right, I'll talk to Weber about getting you paid."

"So then, we aren't getting paid if Weber is going to make the final decision. He'll make a statement about budget cuts and you'll be off the hook."

"My hands are tied, Jim. He has to make the decisions on payments to outside contractors." I could tell he was trying not to laugh.

"So, I'm an outside contractor now. Well, just don't ask for a favor anytime soon." I hung up on him. I knew that would bug him, so I did it. I stood and went to the front to see what Lacey was up to. I found Lynn talking to Lacey and they turned to me.

"Hey Lynn, how's your case on the missing daughter going?" I asked.

"Finished it off in one afternoon. Caught a kidnapper and human trafficker."

"You didn't charge for this, did you?"

She grinned and said, "No. It was so simple, and over before we knew it. I couldn't charge a father who just got his daughter back."

"You seem to be the pro-bono queen of this firm," I said with a laugh. "But that's okay."

"I had to come back here to turn in my report. Now I'm going to pick up my baby girl and go home to play with her."

"Give her a kiss for me." I said, then excused myself and went out to the back to see what Buck and Fred were up to.

I was amazed when I stepped out the back door. The flower garden they had created changed the entire look of the back lot. "Well, this is very nice." I said moving away from the building so I could see the whole landscaping of the flower beds they set up.

"This is totally amazing," I said as I stood looking at all the flowers and plants. The trees really set it off. "Fred, I'm pleased with this. I like the trees."

"My dog needs a place to pee," he said with a sly grin.

"Yes, he does. Well Buck, you and Fred did good today. You should take some pictures and send them to the Review-Journal for their home and garden section." I said.

"I just may do that." Buck said. "Now I have some investigating to do. Fred, the place is now yours to keep up."

I turned to Fred and said, "We have enough information to help catch the Trick-or-Treat Killer, thanks to you. Telling us about the tunnels helped a lot."

"Glad I could help. I hope you catch him, he gives homeless people a bad name."

I smiled but didn't laugh. I figured he was being serious.

~~*~~

"Why did you have to murder Jeff? I about shit my pants when that P.I. told us." Ralph said to Tony in the dingy apartment that Ralph had maintained for Tony all these years.

"I just wanted to settle a score with him, the dirty little liar," Tony spoke, lying on the bed. "I held off long enough, I wanted him dead."

"It's bad enough you've murdered almost every mother in the group, but now Jeff. The police are investigating his murder. One kill a year is something they can't handle. But if you put up too many kills, they will start to put things together."

"Relax, I didn't leave any evidence, just as I didn't for all the other murders."

"You mean the mothers?"

Trick or Treat Murders

Tony grinned and said, "I may have honed my killing skills with a couple other murders throughout the year."

"What? You've committed other murders? Why?" Ralph was in a panic now. "Do you know if they catch you, I'm going down too?"

"Ralph, when you came to me that year after I wasted my sweet mother and asked me to do yours, I began to like the thrill of the kill. I enjoyed the sound of my gun as it blasted the women of my so-called friends. I only let you in on my fake death because you were the only friend I had. And I knew your mother was abusing you, too."

"Yes, and she was as bad as yours. The other mothers were your idea, not mine."

"I hated all those boys, I wanted to make them hurt. Taking out their mothers was my revenge for the way they treated me. Their mothers were all so nice and sweet to them, they didn't deserve to have their mothers. Baking cookies and fudge for them, disgusting. Besides, it was a thrill to hide in the bushes waiting for just the right moment to go up to the house and call Trick-or-Treat. I gave them the trick."

Ralph stood staring at the man on the bed looking so causal about murder. Ralph started to wonder if this was all worth it. He only let the murders of the women over the years go on because he had Tony murder his own mother, at his request. He was as bad as Tony.

"I only let this go all these years because of the secret we shared, but I'm getting nervous about this. Maybe you should stop. The police are on to you, they know you're alive."

"I hope you aren't going to spoil my fun by telling them where I am." Tony got up and pulled the .38 from the crate next to the bed. "I've added something. It's a silencer. So no one will hear you die," Tony said as he aimed and shot Ralph.

"One more problem out of the way." He said smiling.

*

Chapter 22

It was the morning of October 30th, the start of Devil's Night, or Angel's Night, depending on your faith and preference. I didn't worry about Devil's Night, we never had kids come by our home to soap our windows or TP the trees. The security alarms for the property usually kept any hardcore vandals from getting near the house.

I was driving to my building, Penny had gone off to her studio to tape her show. She took Willy with her, which was good, he'd just get into mischief with Fred's dog. Fred hadn't named the dog yet. He said a good name would come to him when it was time. I was looking to the skies and seeing something that didn't happen very often in the Vegas Valley—very dark storm clouds.

It was getting much darker and I knew storms could hit very fast here. The flooding would be right behind. I hoped Fred's friendlies had warned the tunnel people about the impending storm. I was concerned for those in the tunnels now. I'd seen news casts of when it flooded, and the water was like a raging river through the low areas. I've seen cars floating down the freeway. They showed video of the floods streaming into the tunnels, and I never thought about people being in them.

I arrived at the building just as the rain started to come down. It was moderately heavy, but that was just the start. I entered the back door just as it started to come down harder. I was glad I wasn't out in it today.

I saw Buck standing by the storeroom and wondered what he was up to. He looked to me, pulling a note from the storeroom door, and said, "Jim, Fred went out to the tunnels to help his friends get out. I don't like that idea."

I didn't either. "Let's get over to his tunnel and see if he's all right." I was worried now and went by Earl's door. He was in relaxing.

"Earl, follow me and Buck. We may have a problem." I said in a hurry.

He jumped up and came after me. We got to the back door and I quickly explained the situation.

"Damn, let's go then," he said, and we went back out into the storm, which had gotten worse. The wind was blowing heavily, making it difficult to get to our cars. I told everyone to get into my Crown Vic. It was a very heavy car, built like a tank. I drove carefully out onto Industrial Road, it was already flooding along the curbs.

151

Trick or Treat Murders

We navigated over to where Fred's tunnel was and I pulled up by the fenced area. I could see people standing in a nearby sheltered bus stop. A few of them had carts, probably filled with their only possessions. I didn't see Fred or Henry with them. We jumped out of the car and went to the fence, pulled back the wire, and went through. I could see the water running down the canal into the tunnel, the deluge having already reached the halfway point of the concrete walls.

We stopped because it was foolish to go any further as the water rose. I went as close to the river's edge as I dared, and looked into the tunnel to see if I could see anything. It was too dark, visibility was nil.

Earl came up next to me. He yelled over the noise of the storm and the roaring water, "Jim, it's no good to even think about finding him in there. These tunnels flow out of the city. We'd never find him now."

I just stood there choking up. I was so hoping he got out through another tunnel.

"Are you sure he came here?" Buck yelled.

"You had the note saying he was going to help his friends. This is his tunnel, or was," I replied. "He would have come here to help Henry and the couple we met."

"Damn, this is not good," Buck said. "No sense in standing in the rain. Let's sit in the car until the storm passes."

I knew there was no point to standing around getting soaked, which we already were. I turned and we went back to the car. We sat there waiting. The storms could stop as fast as they started. This storm just wasn't going to stop, it seemed to me. Then suddenly, about fifteen minutes later, it ceased and moved away. We got back out and went over to the tunnel. The water was about a foot from the top of the tunnel, not enough room to safely get out. We waited as the water receded. I told Buck and Earl that we would wait until it was safe to go in.

About an hour later, we were sitting by the embankment on a pile of concrete, the water had finally receded to a small stream. I stood and we went down to the tunnel again. I carefully entered, Buck got the flashlights from the car and handed them to us. We were about fifty feet into the tunnel when we heard a voice behind us. I turned, hoping it was Fred. It wasn't.

"What are you looking for?" An older man asked. "The tunnel's been cleaned out, the water pushes most everything not chained down out to Lake Mead."

"Do you know Fred..." I paused, as I just

realized I didn't know Fred's last name.

"Fred Jarvis, old man who lived in this tunnel. Friends with Henry?" the man said.

"Yeah, him. Have you seen him?"

"Nope, I got here just now to see if anyone needed help getting back into the tunnel. I'm what is called a friendly, I warn them when the storms are coming and then help with cleanup." He paused. "If Fred came back into the tunnel and he wasn't out with the rest of them up top, then he either didn't get back here or was taken by the water. If the water got him, he's gone."

"You haven't seen his friend Henry?" I asked.

"Nope, he wasn't up top either."

People were starting to enter the tunnel. I asked them if they saw Fred or Henry. One woman said she saw Fred going into the tunnel. That was not good news for me.

I looked down into the darkness of the tunnel, hoping to see Fred coming out of the gloom. He didn't.

"Let's go back, guys. There's nothing more we can do here." We went to the car and drove back to the office. In the parking lot, we sat in the car looking at Fred's garden. I was trying not to choke up again. Buck quietly cursed and got out of the car. Earl asked if I was alright.

"No, I'm going to sit here for a bit. I'll be in shortly." Earl got out and went into the building.

It just wasn't fair. To get out of those damn tunnels and into a better life, and then this. I sat there for what seemed a long time, wondering if I should call Penny. I decided to wait until I saw her later. I finally got up the strength to get out of the car and went to the building, looking at the flowers and plants that somehow survived the downpour. They were standing tall and straight. The way Fred would have liked them to be.

I opened the back door and went in. I saw everyone standing in the hallway talking aloud to each other. I wondered what was going on. Then they saw me and parted. There was Fred, standing in the middle of the hall, dripping wet.

*

Chapter 23

I ran to him and grabbed him in a bear hug. I pushed back and said, "What the hell happened? Talk to me."

He looked like hell, I apologized and said to go sit down. He went out to the lobby followed by everyone else. He stopped and said, "I'm sorry, I'm getting water all over the place."

"So am I, don't worry about it. Sit." I moved him to the couch and sat next to him. "Now talk to me."

Fred took a breath and said, "I was working on the new flower beds in the front and I could see the clouds gathering. I knew something was going to happen. I left the note and walked over to the tunnel." He took another breath and continued. "I got there just after the rain hit and the water was about ankle deep in the tunnel. I went in and most of the people had left. I asked one straggler where Henry was. He said he didn't know. I went to my old area and could see Henry had packed a number of things and his shopping cart was gone."

He paused, I told him to take his time. I looked

around the lobby. Buck, Earl, Lacey, and Tracey were either standing or sitting, listening.

"I knew Henry didn't pass me on my way in. That told me he went the wrong way. Henry could get lost in the tunnels if the people weren't watching him. I went further into the tunnel, I shouldn't have. The water was already up to my knees. I yelled for him but he didn't respond. I decided to go further and found his shopping cart, but no Henry. He wasn't a strong man, I figured he slipped and the water…" He choked a little.

I looked to Lacey, "Get one of those little bottles of whiskey in your bottom drawer." She gave me a surprised look. "Stay out of my drawers," she said and went to get one. I yelled to her to bring a couple. She came back and handed four to me. I twisted the top off one and handed it to Fred. He smiled and downed it. I did one also. I gave the other two to Buck and Earl. We were all still wet and needing it.

"I was turning to go back out," Fred continued, "but the water was getting deeper. It was up to my waist. I couldn't fight the current, I slipped and it swept me away. I thought I was a goner. Then I saw a weak light ahead coming from above. It was from holes in a manhole. I guided myself over to the side and grabbed onto the ladder coming down. I climbed up, but the water was rising quickly. The manhole access was built up above the tunnel and I hoped the water wouldn't go that high. I couldn't push the manhole, it was too heavy for me. I held on to the ladder forever, breathing air from the holes in the manhole cover. Then the water started to recede. I climbed down and left the tunnel quickly."

"We went to find you." I said. "You must have been in the tunnel while we stood outside. I'm surprised we didn't run into you coming out."

"You must have left before I got out. I was quite a ways in. I came back here and in through the front door. I'm sorry about the water on the floor."

I smiled and said, "It'll get cleaned up, don't worry. Just rest now."

Buck had gone into the back and came up with Fred's dog. The pup came over to Fred and stood up for him. Fred smiled and picked him up.

"I have a name for him now— Henry."

I could see a tear in his eye. "Okay everyone, back to work, we have an office to run and criminals to catch." I stood and helped Fred up. "When you feel up to it, you have gardening to finish and flowers to fix that got hit from the storm."

Fred smiled and stood holding Henry, and went through the doors to the back. I stood in the lobby and watched him through the glass doors as he went into the storeroom. He came out shortly after with the leash for the dog, then went out the back door.

~~*~~

Deacon got a call about a dead body off the strip area in a dumpster. The first responders said they got a 911 call about a body found in the dumpster by a kitchen employee at the Flamingo Hotel Casino. Deacon asked if the man was identified. The officer on the phone said the ID on the body said he was Ralph Reslen. That perked up Deacon as it sounded familiar. He thought back to names given him in the last few days and the questioning of the sons came to mind. He suddenly remembered him. Deacon told the officer he'd be right out. He hung up then made a call.

~~*~~

"Are you sure it's the same man?" I asked Deacon through the speaker of my desk phone. Earl was sitting in my office listening.

"How many Ralph Reslens do you know who are recently involved in this case?"

"Okay, point taken. Where is the body now?" I asked.

Trick or Treat Murders

"In a dumpster behind the Flamingo Hotel. Kitchen staff found him. I'm heading there now, if you'd care to join me to give your ID on him." Deacon's voice came out of the phone speaker.

"I'll be there with my team shortly."

"Team? You have a team? When did that happen?" I could tell he was snickering.

"Never mind. I'll see you there," I said and hung up. I looked at Earl and said, "Okay, team, ready to go?"

He grinned and stood. "Ready to go, team leader. I'll wait by your car."

I went to tell Lacey I was going out with Earl, then headed out to my car. The rain had cleaned the air, it felt pleasant. The humidity disappeared quickly, one reason I liked living here, no humidity. Hot, but dry. Earl was at my car watching the skies.

"Looking for more rain?" I asked him.

He frowned and said, "Just thinking about the people who don't make it out of the tunnels."

"We can't save them all. Most don't want our help. We just have to accept that and help those who want something better." I looked over to Fred who was coming around the building carrying a flat of flowers. He saw us and smiled. His dog was following him with the leash attached to Fred's belt.

"Okay, let's go before Deacon gets impatient." We got in the car and I drove over to the Flamingo Hotel Casino near the corner of Flamingo Road and the strip. I remembered back when I used to work there for Nick North, the comedian who was spending time in prison, entertaining the convicts. He did a whole lot of bad things and he got caught, thanks to my team. I smiled at the thought, my team. I started out with Buck, then Earl, and finally Trapper, before we moved to Vegas. Now we had Lynn, we *were* a team.

I pulled around the back of Harrah's Imperial Palace where water was still flowing down the back drive from the parking structure. I went next door to the back of the Flamingo Hotel where we saw the police vehicles. I pulled up and Earl and I went to the yellow tape. The officer knew us and let us pass. I found Deacon and he asked me to identify the body. I went over and they pulled back the top of the dumpster and I looked in.

"Yep, that's Ralph. Strange, he looks posed."

*

Chapter 24

"He was," came a voice from around the side of the dumpster. It was Joe Lang, county coroner. He came around to us and said, "You can't see it down under the trash, I checked, and when we bring him up, you'll find that he's glued to a stool and has a dead pigeon glued to his hand."

"He's a dead stool pigeon?" Earl asked, trying not to laugh.

"That's my assumption," Joe replied, also trying not to laugh.

"But Ralph didn't say anything to me yesterday that would have given Hall away," I said.

"You're assuming this was Hall's work?" Deacon asked.

"Well, think about it. He was one of Hall's classmates, he talked to us yesterday and now he's dead. I'll bet he was shot."

Joe Lang said, "You'd win that bet. When I dig the bullet out of him, it will most likely match the ones from our Trick-or-Treat Killer." He signaled to his men and they went about pulling Reslen out of the dumpster. We stood back.

After they lifted him out, they put him on the ground, still sitting on the small stool. He looked oddly strange glued to the stool with bird in hand. I was trying not to laugh myself.

"So, is Hall trying to tell us something? If he talked to Ralph before he shot him, then he knows that we know he's alive." I said.

"He has one more woman to kill, then he's done with the list. Maybe he's getting bold and striking out since we know it's him." Deacon said.

"If so, then he'll get careless," I said. "If he talked with Ralph, does that mean they knew each other? Could Ralph have known that Hall was still alive? Maybe a good idea to check into him. See if there's anything that connects lately to Hall."

"I'll get Warren on it. He loves doing the computer stuff." He went away from us and pulled his cell phone.

Earl looked at me and said, "Is Hall tying up loose ends with Ralph Reslen and that guy they found in the desert?"

"Jeff the shoe thief? I'm wondering the same. I

hope he's not going after the men who did him wrong now."

"If Hall knows we know he's alive, will he attempt to murder the Lowbrill woman? Maybe Ralph warned him about that."

"Or Hall was worried that Ralph would tell us where he was. It's all speculation right now."

Deacon came back and said he had Greg Warren checking on Reslen. The coroner's men were putting Reslen in the back of the ME's van as Joe watched them.

"Some rain we had today," Deacon said.

"You don't know the half of it," I said and gave Deacon a quick rundown of Fred's adventure.

"Wow, I'll bet you were crapping bricks," Deacon said.

"To say the least, but all is well now. I just have to keep Fred away from the tunnels." I smiled and looked to Earl. "Shall we go back to base now, team member?"

"You got it, team leader." He grinned and we said so long to Deacon. We went to the car and I stopped next to it.

"What?" Earl asked.

"I have a feeling that Hall is somewhere watching us. This was a big deal to prepare Reslen on the stool and get him in the dumpster. He'd most likely want to watch us." I was looking around the area and couldn't see anyone standing or watching.

"You may be right, but by now he's gone, since they took Reslen away."

"Maybe I'm getting paranoid. Halloween is tomorrow night, it always spooks me out. Hall coming back from the dead and killing women one a year, this is got to be the strangest case I've had. Well, let's go."

~~*~~

Tony Hall laughed and carefully walked from the back of the Flamingo out to Las Vegas Boulevard, AKA 'The Strip' and turned north on the sidewalk. He was going to take his time walking back to the room in the motel that he lived in for the last nine years, after he moved out of the tunnels. Back when he confronted Reslen about killing the man's mother. Hey, Ralph asked him to do it. He was as guilty as Hall. He used that to blackmail Ralph into providing a nice warm place to stay.

Trick or Treat Murders

The motels didn't care who rented the smaller apartments as long as the rent was paid. Ralph always came across with the money. He is, or was, a big shot corporate lawyer. He made enough money to support Hall. Of course, now that Ralph was dead, he'd have to speed up his plan. One last kill, then he was done.

~~*~~

Earl and I arrived at the back parking lot of the office building and I saw Penny's car. She was standing admiring the flower beds, but Fred was nowhere in sight. I knew I shouldn't worry, but I did. Maybe I could put one of those trackers on him— now that was a stupid idea.

"Hey babe," I said, going over to my beautiful wife.

She smiled at me. "This is really fantastic. Fred did a great job."

"Have you been here long?"

"Just got here," she replied.

"Come on in, I have a story to tell you."

Earl said hi to Penny as he entered the building, followed by us. I took Penny to my office and sat her down explaining the events of the morning. She sat staring wide-eyed at what I had to tell her.

"That was nice of Fred to worry about his friend. It's a shame Henry's gone." She went quiet for a moment, I didn't interrupt her. "Have you caught your killer yet?"

"Nope, and he's killing more people now." I told her about the dead stool pigeon in the dumpster. She laughed.

"I'm sorry for the poor man, but it is funny." She got serious and asked, "Are you hungry?"

"Yes, I am. It's been a busy morning and I could use a good meal. What say I find Fred and we take him to Angelo's for lunch?"

"Works for me."

I stood and went out to find Fred. He was busy in front of the building arranging a couple trees.

"Fred, take a break. My wife and I are taking you to lunch."

He grinned and picked up his dog, following me into the building. Penny was in the lobby and went to Fred when we entered. She was playing with the dog's head as Willy was trying to get out of his new doggy purse. We never did go back to recover his old purse.

Fred put his dog in the store room, as Penny gave Willy to Lacey, then we went back out to the car.

We drove over to Mama Mia, parked and got out. I stood looking at the front of the restaurant and thought that maybe it could use a few flowers and trees. I told Fred, he smiled and studied the front of the building.

"Think you could do something with this place?"

"I'm sure I can. If the owner doesn't mind."

"Well, I'm part owner here. I'm sure we won't mind."

We went in and Angelo came over to us with his big smiling face. "Mr. and Mrs. R, so good to see you." He looked at Fred and got a strange look on his face. "Fred?"

Fred looked surprised and said, "Angelo?"

*

Chapter 25

Angelo went to Fred and got him in a bear hug. They stood apart and Angelo said, "Fred! I can't believe it's you!"

I was surprised, to say the least. "You two know each other?"

Angelo grinned and said, "Sure do, I knew Fred back when my real father ran numbers in Newark, out in New Jersey. Fred was a bag man, but when my father was murdered, he left to go work for a family out here in Vegas at some casino. We lost touch."

"Fred, you worked for the mob?"

"I told you that I did when I was in the cash room at the casino. That's why I was let go, being part of the family, the new casino owners didn't want me working there. Angelo was a friend when I worked with the DeMarko family. I hated to leave them, but I got a better offer and a warmer climate out here."

"Come, all my friends, this is a special occasion," Angelo led us to a table by the fireplace, which wasn't on. He snapped his fingers to a couple waitpersons and they came flying over. Angelo didn't tolerate slow employees. "Get my friends anything they want and make sure to tell the cooks that it's special for me." We gave our food orders and they went off.

Angelo sat and asked Fred to tell him what he had been up to. Fred hesitated to tell him about his homelessness, but gave details of what happened after he lost his job at the casino. He talked and we listened, up to when he was helped by me.

Angelo looked over to me and said, "I've always said you is good people, Mr. R."

Our meals came and I asked Angelo, "Is my daughter working?"

"No, she works tonight. I'll tell her you were here." Angelo looked so happy to find an old friend. I often wondered how he felt being in Vegas having no family or friends from his past. Now he did.

Angelo stood and said to enjoy our meals. "I'll see you later, I have business to do." He went off.

I asked Fred, in between putting food into my mouth, "Why didn't you get hold of Angelo when you lost your job?"

"I tried, but after his father was murdered, his

family started to fall apart and I couldn't find them."

"I remember Angelo telling me something about that time. They moved to Mississippi, or somewhere down there, and Angelo's mother married some mob capo named Mangelo. He was knocked off and then Angelo's mom married another capo named Traviano. They're up in New York now. Too bad you couldn't find him back then."

"Well, it's all coming together now. I think it was your little dog Willy who saved me. If I hadn't found him that day, none of this would have happened."

I looked at Penny, she had a big smile.

We finished our meals and Angelo came back to us. "Mr. R, do you mind if I take Fred away from you for a while. I'll bring him back to you, after we reminisce."

"If it's alright with Fred, it's fine with me." I said. He agreed.

Fred said, as we were going to the exit, "Please see that Henry is fed."

"I will, now don't you stay out too late young man," I said with a smile. He laughed and Penny and I left after thanking Angelo for the great meal.

Trick or Treat Murders

~~*~~

Tony was sitting in Jeff's car that he took after he murdered him. He was near the office of Richards Investigations and said to himself. "So, this is where Ralph found out the information about me. I need to visit the great P.I. and see how much he knows about me. I don't want him spoiling my one big final kill."

~~*~~

Penny and I got back to the building and she went in. I walked around the side of the building to see what Fred had accomplished. I wasn't checking up on him, I was marveling at what he had done. I saw a car parked down the road, but didn't think much about it. I was out front looking as I heard the car start up and slowly drive by the office. I turned and tried to see the driver. I could swear he looked familiar. Then my cell phone buzzed. It was Deacon.

I answered as I watched the car drive away. "What's up?" I asked.

"Got some info for you. It seems Ralph was paying a monthly rental bill to a motel up east of the Fremont Street area. I think he may have provided

Hall with a place to live. Care to go take a look?"

"Give me the address and I'll meet you there." He did and I went through the front door and quickly explained to Penny where I was going. I went out the back door to the car and was out on the road.

I arrived after negotiating the traffic on the strip. I saw Deacon and two patrol cars out front of the motel. Deacon waved to me as I pulled up. I went to him and he said he was going to the office to see which room could be Hall's. He told the four cops to spread out and watch the front, to make sure Hall didn't escape.

We entered the motel office and saw a middle-aged woman looking out the window at the cops. She turned to us and said, "What's going on?"

"Ma'am, we just need to know what room a man named Tony Hall is in?"

"Ain't got no Tony Hall living here," she said.

"How about Ralph Reslen? Does he have a room here?" I asked.

She looked more alert, "Yeah, he rents by the month, apartment 14, around the side."

We thanked her and she said, "You ain't going to do any shooting, are ya?"

173

Trick or Treat Murders

Deacon smiled and said, "We hope not." We left the office and Deacon yelled, "Fourteen." and the officers ran around to the door. We all stood ready as Deacon banged on the door, yelling "Police, open up Hall!"

There was no response. We jumped when a voice came from behind us. "Don't you break down that door!" It was the woman from the office. "Fool cops, always busting doors," she said as she walked up to the door with a passkey. Deacon grabbed it from her and pulled her away, handing her off to an officer standing behind him. Deacon stood next to the door and carefully put the key in the lock. He turned the knob and pushed it open. No gun fire came from the room.

Deacon peeked carefully around the door and saw nothing in the tiny one room apartment. The bathroom door was open and he could see no one in it. The cops all streamed in on his signal and secured the room.

"Well, he's not here." Deacon was checking objects on the dresser and held up a burlap bag with two holes cut out for eyes. "Looks like we found his hideout," he said with a big smile.

"Great, but where's Hall?" I asked. I turned to look out the door to the parking lot of the motel. By the road I could see a car. The same make and model of the one that had cruised past my office. I had that tingle.

*

Chapter 26

"Uh, Deacon, come over here, please," I said as I watched the car. It still sat there, the passenger just watching. He had sunglasses on now, and I couldn't see his face that well.

"What's the matter?" he asked.

I pulled him over to the window and moved the curtain back a little. "See that red car out on the street?"

"Yeah."

"It's the same car that cruised by my office about twenty minutes ago. It either followed me here or the driver knew to come here. Get my drift?"

"Yeah, I get it." He turned to the men in the

room, now wondering what we were up to. He explained to them, "I want everyone to casually walk out to their cars, drive out and then we will go after the red car out there. Any questions?"

They had none, so Deacon let them go out in twos. After the first two were in their car and the second pair got into theirs, Deacon and I left the room, sending the lady manager back to her office, thanking her for her help. Deacon closed the door as the officers started their cars. I was carefully watching the red car, it hadn't moved. We got into Deacon's car and slowly drove out. When we hit the street, Deacon hit the sirens and lights, followed by the two patrol cars. We had to drive around a median, during that time the red car took off and was moving away from us.

The three cars were in pursuit and Deacon sent out a call for back up on the roads. The red car was moving fast, but Deacon's Charger Interceptor kept up.

"So, we keep chasing him until one of us runs out of gas?" I asked.

"I got a full tank. That's a Pontiac GTO. I'm sure it has a good sized tank. We'll just have to force him off the road."

"Where's he heading for out here? This is the area where he murdered the women," I said. I thought about it and then it came to me. The tunnels. "He's heading for the tunnel, by where he faked his death. I'll just bet you on that."

"If he gets into the tunnels, I'm not going in after him," Deacon said.

"Chicken," I said.

We drove on, all three of the police units jockeying to get around him, but he kept moving in the way. Luckily, the road was sparse of traffic and what there was moved out of the way quickly. Then I saw it ahead. The fenced area for the drain culvert leading to a tunnel. The same place where Hall faked his death.

"If he does manage to get into the tunnel, we may as well forget going after him. I assume he's had a few years to get to know the tunnel system. We'd never find him," I said, just as the GTO jumped the curb and rammed the fence. The car drove down the embankment, and as we arrived, I could see it stopped at the mouth of the tunnel. The driver's door was open and Hall was gone. "Damn!"

"There he goes. We are back to the beginning," Deacon said as he turned off his siren and flashers. The two patrol cars pulled up next to us and waited.

Deacon got out and the officers came around to him. "I want you men to go into the tunnel and bring him out," he said, then grinned. They looked at him like he was crazy. "I'm kidding. We may as well go back to the motel and see what we can find there."

Deacon was quiet on the way back to the motel. I asked, "What's going through that huge head of yours?"

He smiled, "I was thinking about how a person could do this horrible deed every year and not feel any guilt."

"Not everyone thinks like you or me. We have feelings and we worry about others. Some people just don't give a rat's rear about others. Serial killers are not wired in their heads like we are," I said.

"I realize that. It's just that I'm still surprised. We can watch Lowbrill and if Hall is determined to get to her, we should be able to nab him."

"I'll take that on faith. We do need to get hold of him before he murders again. Now he's hitting people not on the 'mom list'. Maybe you should warn the other guys from his class."

"I'll have Warren contact them to say that Reslen was murdered and to be careful. That's the best I can do without dragging them all into protective custody."

"Whatever, it's getting late and I'm beat. After

178

thinking Fred died in the flood and finding out Fred and Angelo are old friends, then chasing Hall, I'm wasted."

"You old people are like that," Deacon said with a sideways glance.

"Thank you, Bunny Bear," I said with a serious look.

Deacon just huffed and pulled into the parking lot of the motel. My car was still parked there and I told Deacon I was going home.

"Okay, tomorrow we hopefully nab Hall," he said

"I hope so. I'll call in the morning." I left him standing by the car as the other two patrol cars pulled into the lot. I got in my car and drove out. Fred was with Angelo, I hoped they weren't getting into any trouble. Two old mob wise guys, I hope I didn't get any calls to bail them out. I wasn't sure where Penny was, I left her at the office. I pulled my cell phone at a light and pushed the speed dial, then set it to speaker. I put it in the phone cradle on my dashboard and waited while it rang.

"Hello? Are you finished chasing crooks?" she asked.

"For now I am. I was on my way home and I

wondered where you were."

"I'm at home, waiting. It's Devil's Night and I'm feeling very devilish. I hope you aren't too worn out."

"I'll be there shortly. Are you wearing the red outfit with the horns?"

"I am."

"I'm hurrying."

~~*~~

Tony stumbled through the darkness of the tunnel. He didn't figure they would follow him in. Unfortunately, he didn't have a flashlight, so he had to feel his way in the dark. Down a ways he saw a light. It came from one of the homeless who were camping there and they had a lantern. Tony moved closer as a man stood and asked, "Who are you?" He was holding a baseball bat, weapon of choice for many of the people who lived there.

"I need your light. I have to get to another tunnel I know of that leads out."

"Go back the way you came, it leads out, too. I can't give you my lamp. I'll be in the dark."

Tony pulled the .38 from his belt and shot the man in the leg. With the silencer, the only noise was the man crying out in pain.

"Sorry, I really need the light." Tony went and took the light from a crate and went into the tunnel further. The man was lying on the ground, but the bullet had only grazed just below his knee. The darkness may have prevented Tony from doing more damage. The man pushed himself up with the bat and struggled to go out the way Tony came in.

Tony moved quickly into the tunnels he knew well. Now he had to escalate his plan. Tomorrow night was Halloween.

*

Chapter 27

Penny was extremely devilish and I didn't complain. After we came out of the bedroom, we were resting on the couch in the living room with beer and chips. We hadn't done this in a while, so it felt nice. We were watching "World War Z" on the 3D TV I had bought for the living room and we were enjoying the zombies chasing Brad Pitt around. I was hoping they'd eat him, Penny wanted to eat him herself.

My cell phone buzzed and it was Deacon, according to the caller ID. I paused the movie, put the phone on speaker and said, "Did you catch Hall already?"

"Not yet, but we have the plan all in place. I have a police woman dressed as a witch with lots of Kevlar under her gown. She'll answer the door with make-up on so Hall shouldn't know it's not Lowbrill."

"You hope, but sounds like a good plan though. Where will everyone else be?"

"We will be in costumes walking around the

subdivision. Lynn wanted to get me a bear costume with bunny ears, I told her to not even think about it."

I was laughing at the thought of him in the suit. "So what are you dressing as?"

"I'm not dressing. I need to maintain some decorum as a police officer." Deacon laughed. "But I hope Hall doesn't see through us. He does know we're watching for him. I don't know how he will get to Lowbrill, but if this is his last mother, he may shoot her and go out in a blaze of gun fire with us."

"Whatever. This is going to end well or badly. But either way, you should get Hall. Just wear your vest so he doesn't shoot you."

"Lynn is insisting on it, and I don't want to get her stirred up. I'll see you tomorrow, I'm sure you'll want to be part of the sting."

"Of course, I'll be dressed as Batman," I said with a laugh as Penny poked my rib. "See you tomorrow." I took the phone off speaker and hung up.

The movie ended and Penny said she was going to bed. They had a special Halloween segment on her show tomorrow, and she had to go in early to get into her costume.

"What are you going to be dressed as?" I asked.

Trick or Treat Murders

"I'm not telling, you'll see when you get home or if I come to the office first. I'll probably come to the office, since you'll be trick-or-treating with a murderer later."

She went to the bedroom as I closed up the TV and put away our 3D glasses. I went to the bedroom followed by Willy, then got ready and crawled into bed, hoping I didn't dream about zombies.

The next morning came fast and I had no zombie dreams, thankfully. Penny had gone off to work, taking Willy with her. I did my morning ritual and headed to the office.

I came in the back door and went up to the front where I found Fred in the lobby with Lacey. They were laughing, something I liked to see Lacey do. She usually seemed sour, but occasionally I could make her laugh. It was good to see Fred could do it too.

"What are you two discussing?" I asked.

Fred turned to me and told me about his night with Angelo and the strip club they went to. I told Fred if I had known that, I would have joined them. Of course, Penny would have insisted on joining us.

"Glad you had a nice time and found an old friend," I said.

"Angelo is quite a guy, we used to get into heaps of trouble back in Jersey."

I could imagine. I turned to Lacey and asked who all was in.

"Buck is in his office, as is Lynn. Earl slipped in the back door and is in his office. Now Trapper has been missing for the last three days, but I do remember him saying he was going out of town with Samantha."

"So everyone important is here, then?"

"You could say that, but not to Trapper," she said with a laugh.

"I'm going to see Earl. You two keep having fun." I went back through the glass door to the hallway and down to Earl's office. He was sitting at his desk, talking on the phone. He waved me in when he saw me and I sat in the chair next to his desk and waited. He was talking to his lady friend, Paula, I figured from his conversation. Paula had agreed to babysit for Lynn and Deacon, an arrangement that Earl wasn't too happy with, but he accepted it. Earl liked his privacy, and with a baby in the house it was difficult. That's why Earl spent so much time in the office. He finished the call.

"So, what's on the agenda for tonight?" he asked.

Trick or Treat Murders

"Lots of candy and maybe a big treat. I talked to Deacon and they are getting ready to catch Hall. I just hope it works out."

"Think positively. Hall will screw up now that we understand him. He's a nut case and won't think straight now that we are watching for him. He'll go for the kill and he'll screw up."

"I'm glad you're confident about this. I think it may end badly. Hall has lots of experience slipping up to houses and shooting women." I said.

"That's something I wondered about. How did Hall get the women alone to kill? Where were their husbands or kids? Halloween is a big deal to most families."

"Most men take the kids out for Halloween and the wife stays home giving out candy, I figure. Or Hall was real patient with some of them and waited until the right moment to swoop in."

"Whatever, are you going to watch the take down?"

"I'll be there. We invested all this work so I want to be there at the end of it all. You can come too, if you want."

"Nope, Paula and I are going to a Halloween

party for some friends. I don't want to have murder and criminals on my mind tonight. Paula has the same costume Princess Leia wore in the movie with that big slug creature."

"Ooh, the slave girl costume?"

"That's it. I am going as Han Solo, so it should be interesting."

"I never took you as a fan of Star Wars."

"I'm not really, but I like the costumes," he said with a devilish grin.

~~*~~

Tony slipped back into his apartment after watching to make sure the cops were all gone. He went under the yellow tape across the door, and closed the door quickly behind him. Luckily the forensic people didn't take all his things. His clothes were still there, but the bag for his head was gone. No problem, he'd use a pillow case instead. He felt disappointed since the burlap bag was his costume for all these years. He looked around and the place had been dusted and drawers pulled apart. There was not much that they had to find, so he was not worried that they'd find anything important. He went to the drawer in the cheap dresser and found his extra bullets were gone. No problem he thought, he had enough on him to deal with this night. He pulled a chair over and climbed up. He pushed a ceiling panel over and reached up. He found the package he would need to take out the one person who he wanted dead the most.

*

Chapter 28

I left Earl's office and went to mine. I sat at my desk and wondered what to do for the day until it was time for the night's events. I could meditate, but I wasn't tired, I had just gotten out of bed. I had no reports to file, I finished them all up to keep Lacey happy. I picked up the remote for the TV and went to turn it on but it didn't start. I looked at the TV hanging on the wall and could see the cord was unplugged. I went over and found a note taped to it. "Do not plug this in or Penny will murder you, thank you, Lacey."

Bob Moats

I had the feeling that Penny didn't want me to see her on her show in her Halloween costume before she came in. Now I was really lost. I went back to my desk and opened up my computer and started up the Word program. I opened the Dropbox folder and extracted the latest file of the new book I was writing. Dropbox was nice, I could save my book files at home in the folder and they'd be on my computer at work. I didn't trust the Cloud, but it was nice to have the files anywhere I went with a computer.

I worked on my latest book for a while, until Lacey buzzed me on the desk phone. That surprised me, as she usually came to my door. I answered and she said I had someone on the office line who wanted to talk to me. I presumed it was someone who didn't know my cell phone number. Which was fine with me. I thanked her and pushed the first blinking line button after lifting up the phone and said hello.

"Jim Richards, you are so clever aren't you?"

"Well, I like to think so. Who is this?"

"We've never personally met, but you almost caught me yesterday. You chased me back into my old home in the tunnels."

I suddenly had a shiver. It was Tony Hall calling me. "Well, Tony, are you calling to surrender to me?" I was trying to stay calm as I flipped on the switch to record the call.

189

Trick or Treat Murders

"Don't count on it. I have a mission to take care of tonight and you can't stop me. The police won't be able to stop me either, they're just a bunch of bungling clowns."

"I wouldn't be too harsh on them, they do their best. Besides, Ringling Brothers would never hire them. So, what do I owe the honor of your call?"

"I just wanted to gloat. Tonight is going to be my big finale. My big exit stage left finale. I murdered all the mothers so my old school chums would hurt. Tonight, I'll take care of the last problem I wanted to resolve all these years."

"You're going to try and kill Jeff Lowbrill's mother. The last of them. Who are you going to go after next? Politicians, I hope."

"You can joke all you want, Richards. All these years I waited to do away with Jeff, my needs were satisfied with his death. I just have one more."

"What about Ralph Reslen? Were you satisfied to kill your benefactor? The man who paid your way all these years."

"Ralph was an idiot. He asked me to murder his own mother after I revealed myself to him years ago. He hated his mother as much as I hated mine. He was becoming a liability that had to be dealt with. So I eliminated him from the equation."

"So what are you going to do next? Retire to Florida?"

"You'll find out. You people can watch over Lowbrill all you want. I don't care. I'll take out my last victim tonight and you won't stop me. I thought my mother was a monster, but I'm going to slay the dragon tonight."

"Why don't you just give yourself up? You'll never get to Lowbrill," I said, hoping it would be a challenge for him.

"I'm not worried about that bitch, she will be dealt with in the afterlife. I have to get ready before it's trick-or-treat time, I just wanted to call and taunt you a little. Have a nice Halloween, Richards, and goodbye."

He hung up. I shut off the recorder and replayed it, listening to his words carefully. I couldn't get anything from it to tell how he was planning to get to Lowbrill. I just knew he was accepting it as a challenge. I called Deacon and told him about the call and said I had it recorded.

"Can you bring it in so I can hear it?"

"Sure, it's on an SD card, I'll bring it over right now. I was just bored here until the call from Tony."

191

Trick or Treat Murders

We said our goodbyes and I hung up. It was still too early for Penny to come in, so I figured I could go visit Deacon and be back in time to see her costume. I went up front to tell Lacey and then out to my car.

I was sitting in Deacon's office while he and Greg Warren listened to the recording on the computer. It finished and Greg said, "The guy is bold for one thing. Calling to brag about his crime tonight."

"He's a psycho, he lived in the tunnels too long, it must have fried his brain." Deacon said.

"I think the abuse his mother inflicted on him fried his brain. The tunnels just gave him the time to let it fester enough to drive him to murder." I said.

"So Ralph was in on it. He was sure cool when we questioned him." Deacon said.

"Yeah, but he must have been worried that we would find out about his past, too. He probably confronted Hall and pushed Hall into killing him. I have a feeling that getting to Lowbrill is going to be a challenge for him. He wants her as his big farewell." I said.

"The only way Hall is going to get to Lowbrill is with a tank." Warren said.

"We don't want to make it too hard for him to get there. Our objective is to catch him." I said, then stood. "I'm leaving, I have a date with my wife. She dressed up for her Halloween show and wants me to see it. Call me when you're ready to go stake out the house."

I went out to my car and back to my office. I came in the back door, closed the door and found the hallway lights were out. It was dark and I couldn't see where the switch was. Then the lights turned on and there stood Elvira, Mistress of the Dark, standing at the other end of the hall. I about had a heart attack. Then I heard Penny's distinctive giggle. She slithered over to me and I could see now that it was her.

"Wow, they did a great job of making you look like Elvira." I mostly stammered. "Even the big breasts, that's a real good push-up bra." Then I noticed the deep v-cut of the dress, she wasn't wearing a bra. I grinned.

She threw her arms around me and kissed my ear, then licked it. I shivered. "Are you going to be able to wear the outfit all day?" I asked, hopefully.

"Of course, Sweetie, I'm going out trick-or-treating with Lacey and Jessie tonight while you go chase your Halloween killer. But I want you home before midnight."

She licked my ear again and I said, "I'll definitely be there."

*

Chapter 29

She pushed away and said. "I'm going up front to scare customers." She turned and sashayed to the glass doors, her butt wiggling on the way. Damn, I loved how she moved, especially for a sixty-two-year-old woman. Some women her age would be hiding in their homes or having expensive plastic surgeries. Not Penny, she was all natural and still sexy.

I went to see what Earl was up to, he wasn't in, so I went to Buck's office and he was gone too. Lynn was off playing with her daughter, I presumed. Maybe getting ready for the kids to come get the candy. I imagined how hard it must be for Deacon to be away from his baby on her first Halloween. Hopefully, we could get this wrapped up quickly and everyone could go home.

I went to my office to sit and think about what to do tonight. I found if you imagined a scenario, you could plan it out. I was hoping to be the superhero and take out Hall myself, bullets bouncing off my chest. Then Buck walked in, interrupting my daydream.

"Hey, Jim. What's happening with your catching the killer tonight?"

"Deacon has it all arranged for his men to stake out the victim's home. I'm going along to watch it happen. You want to go?"

"I'd love it. I have no plans now that Maria and I are no longer seeing each other, so I'll take crime any day."

"Good, you'll give me company. I got a call from Tony Hall today."

"No way, he called you?"

I reached over and started the call on my computer. Buck sat quietly listening. When it finished he said, "Ballsy guy, isn't he? I don't know, but it seems like he isn't going after Lowbrill. He said something that made me think that."

"Really? You don't think he wants Lowbrill? She's the last of the mothers. It's his final blow to

195

motherhood and his buddies."

"Yeah, but Lowbrill's son is dead, so what's the point of killing her now?"

Buck had me at a loss for words. He was right about that, I guess. "Well, she is the last one on his list. I can't think of anyone else that we came across in our investigation who he wanted dead. Other than the guys from his class."

"Well, I could be wrong, but it sounded like he was after someone else."

"I guess we'll find out tonight. Have you seen Penny in her costume?"

"Yeah, I had to leave the room, she looked too good. I love Elvira." He said, showing his walrus grin.

"So do I, and she knows it. She's teasing me, and I'm not arguing either." My cell phone buzzed, it was Deacon.

"Hey, what's up?" I said as I put him on speaker so Buck could hear. "Buck is here with me."

"I'm going to start the sting. Trick-or-treaters start when it's still light. Most of the time Hall struck under darkness, but he may be changing up since he knows we will be watching tonight."

"Very true, he may even change costume so we don't recognize him. CSI took his mask so he needs something different."

"I can meet you at the precinct, then I'll be taking our men to the house to get ready."

"I'm on my way." I disconnected the phone and said to Buck, "Shall we go?"

We got up and I went to the lobby to say goodbye to Elvira. She looked so good, I made my exit quickly. Buck and I went to my car and drove out.

Everyone was in the squad room listening to Deacon explain the plan. "I have permission from a neighbor across the street to put a sniper in an upstairs window." He looked to the man who was the sniper. "You will be watching the door closely, and if you see a gun come out, shoot."

"Be careful some kid in a cowboy suit doesn't pull his six-shooter." I said. Everyone laughed.

"No, Jim's right. We have to be careful. The police woman who is being made up at the house right now will have a Kevlar vest on and if she gets shot, you'll know it's not some cowboy kid. Use your discretion and listen for my signal. Now, everyone needs to lay low and stay at the houses we have permission to hide in. On my signal, everyone comes running. Okay, everyone knows where they need to be, so go."

"Where are you going to be?" I asked, as the police left the room.

"I'm going to be in the Lowbrill house, I presume you want to join me?"

"That would be a plan. You lead the way and we will follow." I stood and Buck joined me.

We went out to our cars, I took mine as I wanted to leave quickly after they captured Hall—to go see Elvira.

I followed Deacon and we drove into the alley behind the house. We parked in the alley, went through a gate in the fence, and went to the door. The officer standing guard let us in. In the kitchen in the back of the house sat a witch, all green and ugly. It was the woman cop who would be Lowbrill for the night. Deacon got everyone ready and we heard the doorbell. Our first trick-or-treater. The woman cop put on her pointed hat and went out to the door. We stood in the living room next to the door and waited. She looked to us and then opened the door ready for anything.

It was two little ballerinas and they yelled the traditional Halloween chant. The witch gave them each some wrapped candy and they ran off. She closed the door and took off the hat. She said, "I think it's going to be a long night."

We endured four hours of kids begging for candy and the witch was getting itchy in the costume. Deacon asked Lowbrill if she had a fan. The woman went and brought out a box fan and plugged it in. Deacon aimed it at the witch and she hiked up her gown to cool. Luckily she had on pants.

I looked at my watch. "What times did Hall kill all the other mothers?"

Deacon looked to Warren and repeated the question. Warren said, "I had the statistics for the perp and every kill was made between seven and nine."

"Well, it's almost nine now. Where is he?" I asked.

Buck had been sitting quietly on the couch and spoke up, "I tell ya, he's got someone else he's going to murder tonight." Deacon looked at him and asked, "Why?"

"Something he said about not caring for that bitch, referring to Lowbrill, and that she would be judged in the afterlife. Why would she be judged in the afterlife if he was judging her here?"

Trick or Treat Murders

"Okay, it's a stretch, but who else would he murder?" I asked.

"I don't know, he murdered his mother because she abused him. Maybe his father helped her." Buck said.

"Or his father didn't do anything about the abuse. That would make me mad." Deacon said.

"Damn, it may be the father he's after. Hall murdered Jeff Lowbrill, so it's not a priority to murder his mother." I said and stood. "I don't know where his father lives, Earl went there."

Deacon asked Warren to check his info and give us the location. Warren got out his phone, pulled up the files and gave us the address."

Deacon said, "I shouldn't be leaving here on speculation. We may be wrong."

"Buck and I can go. If we find Hall, we'll call you." I looked to Buck and said, "Let's go."

*

Chapter 30

Buck and I drove out of the subdivision and over to the address that Warren had given us. I checked it with the map program on my phone and headed to the father's apartment. We arrived and the lights were either off or the curtains were heavy enough to keep light from showing.

Buck and I went up to the apartment and I quietly told him we should look through windows. I went to the front and Buck went to the back. I couldn't see anything, the curtains were drawn tight. Buck came around to the front and said, "No dice."

We stood there and I said, "We could just knock on the door."

Buck grinned and said that would work. We went to the porch and suddenly heard a crashing noise from inside. I tried the door knob, it wouldn't open. I looked at Buck and said, "I think that's a good reason for breaking and entering." He agreed.

We both had our weapons out and I stood back as Buck moved to crash through the door. He took a big lunge and went through the door easily.

Trick or Treat Murders

Apparently, it wasn't a good door, but Buck managed to catch himself before he hurtled to the floor. I came in behind him with my gun up and didn't immediately see anyone, we moved into the next room.

Tony Hall was standing with his arm around his father's neck and the .38 at his head.

Buck said to me, "I told you he wasn't after Lowbrill."

"Screw Lowbrill, I killed her son, my revenge was satisfied. You aren't too bad, Richards. You found me."

"Actually, it was my partner here, Buck. He figured it out. Now why don't you let your father go and we can all have a nice trip to LVPD."

"I told you on the phone, this was my big finale. I'm going out in a blaze of glory after I waste my dear father."

"Why?" I asked. Tony seemed to enjoy talking about his crimes.

"This bastard just stood around when my wonderful mother would beat me. He did nothing about it. He's spineless and doesn't deserve to live."

"Why did you wait all these years, why didn't

you murder him when you did your mother?"

"I hated her so much and never thought much about this spineless, weak bastard. Over the years of killing all the mothers, I decided I just had to do this. For my last hurrah."

"So, how are you going out in a blaze of glory?" I asked.

He got a strange smile and said, "I'm going to move away from my daddy dearest, now don't shoot, you may regret it." He slowly moved away from his father, and we could see it. He had six sticks of dynamite strapped to his chest. "I stole these from a construction site where they're building some new hotel. The box in my hand is a dead man's switch. If I let it go, the whole thing blows. So, do you still want to shoot me?"

"I'm not ready to die, are you Buck?" I asked my friend.

"Hell, no. Shall we depart this nuthouse?" He smiled at me.

We both slowly moved back and out of the apartment. Hall was screaming for us to get back in the room.

Outside, I said to Buck. "This is not our fight. I'll call Deacon, he can get the bomb squad and a police negotiator to talk to this nut." We moved away from the apartment, we could still hear Hall screaming for us to come back.

We stood in the parking lot as I called Deacon and told him the facts. He said he'd be there shortly.

We were watching the building when we heard Hall loudly call out, "Trick-or-treat!" Then we fell back as the blast of the dynamite blew out the front of the building. Glass and bricks came flying as we tried to dive behind my car. The debris flew everywhere and my ears felt like I'd been boxed by a giant.

Once all the bits and pieces stopped falling, I stuck my head over the car to see the building in flames. I called the fire department and then Deacon and told him what happened. I could barely make out what was said in return because of the ringing in my ears.

Shortly after, Deacon had pulled into the parking lot and ran over to us after he threw his car in park. We all stared at the fire as the firemen were trying to douse the flames.

"Hell, Jim, you couldn't wait for me?"

"Huh? What? My ears are still ringing. Speak up," I said with a grin.

"It's probably old age that causes your hearing loss," he said.

"I heard that." I was laughing and said, "It's all yours now. I got Elvira waiting for me at home." Deacon gave me a strange look. Buck said he would stay and explain.

I was more interested in getting home, than explaining about some serial killer and his death wish. Buck could handle that. I left the parking lot and was on the road to my "Mistress of the Night."

By morning, Penny had managed to at least keep the wig on. Everything else was on the floor. I staggered to my personal bathroom and started the shower. I stepped in and suddenly found another person moving under the water with me. I didn't object.

We both dried off and did our morning routine. Penny went off to work to have the make-up girls remove Elvira from her face. It was pretty much ruined. I kidded her about her make-up looking scary for the day after Halloween, she just beat on me until I ran for cover.

I drove to the office and saw Deacon's car in the lot. I went through the back door and up to the front. Deacon and Lynn were at the counter with Lacey.

Trick or Treat Murders

Deacon smiled and said, "We should make you pay for destruction of the building last night. You should have talked him out of it."

"Deduct it from the payment for my investigations in this case." I said back.

Buck came in and joined us. I said, "It was Buck who helped figure out where Hall was going to be. Too bad the father was a victim of Hall's vendetta."

"Well, it saved Clark County from the expense of a trial for Hall and housing him in prison." Buck said.

"You could look at it that way." I said with a smile.

Fred came through the glass doors and walked up to me. "I'm going to spend the day with Angelo and his lady friend, Sophia. I hope that's all right?"

"Fred, you're a free man, don't ask, tell. Go have fun and stay out of trouble."

He went out the back door to meet with the car Angelo sent to pick him up. I was happy for him.

"So, is Fred part of our team now?" Buck asked.

"He is, if Angelo doesn't steal him away. I think he'll hang around for a while." I replied.

"Good, I like the little man," Buck said and went back to his office.

"So, how was your night of visiting with Elvira?" Lynn asked. "Penny called me about it before she got here yesterday. She had pictures taken at her studio. I can hardly wait to see them."

"Well, I saw her and she looked good. Now, if you'll all excuse me, I will retire to my office." I looked to Lacey. "When Penny comes in, send her to my office immediately. Tell her not to bother knocking."

I laughed evilly and went to my office.

THE END

For every ending, there's a new beginning.

Trick or Treat Murders

Special preview of the next book
"Santa Murders"

Chapter 1

The man liberally applied the spirit gum glue to his chin and cheeks. He wanted to be sure the fake beard wouldn't come loose or fall off. He spread the sticky liquid to his upper lip and then pressed the hairs of the white beard and moustache to his skin. He patted carefully along the edges so the glue didn't ooze out through the hair. He sat back and admired the new look in the mirror of the dressing table. It pleased him. He stood and went to a chair where a "fat suit" hung and pulled it on. His belly was now like a "bowl full of jelly" and he gave a happy laugh that came out, "Ho, ho, ho," and filled the room with his deep voice. He pulled on the red velour pants trimmed nicely with white fur and tightened his belt. Then he pulled on the black boots and lastly, shrugged into a coat of the same velour material as the pants, fully covering his big fake belly.

He stood in front of the full length mirror on the wall and took a cap from the hook next to it and pulled it on his head. He straightened out the bright white wig that was attached to the cap and was satisfied as he turned around in front of the mirror, checking out his outfit. *Perfect,* he thought, a nice disguise for what he was going to do. Very seasonal and something that no one would suspect him of committing crimes in.

He went to a table next to his bed and picked up the .45 caliber handgun and lifted his coat, placing the gun under the belt. He straightened the coat and took one last look in the mirror. Seeing no bulge indicating he was carrying a gun, he was now ready to commit murder.

~~*~~

Penny and I had gotten through the Thanksgiving festivities with all our friends at Angelo's restaurant. I had booked his big banquet room for everyone and had them prepare a special turkey meal with all the trimmings. Everyone in my firm of investigators, along with Deacon and Lynn, were there and having fun. My daughter joined us after she personally made sure all our food was prepared properly. I insisted that Angelo and his lady friend Sophia join us, along with Fred, the new addition to our family.

Fred was settling in with us and I was glad he was out of the homeless life. He was taking care of the building, both cleaning and landscaping, and was our live-in night watchman. He and Buck had fixed up the room in Buck's old office in the store room, turning it into a small living space. I think Buck took a real liking to Fred.

The Thanksgiving feast was a memory now as Penny and I were navigating the Boulevard Mall on 'Black Friday' seeking out presents for Christmas. I wasn't fond of shopping with Penny, she would always make a big production out of it. But this was for Christmas and it was the one time of the year I didn't mind shopping with her. Of course, I'd have to go shopping by myself for gifts for Penny, and I had no idea what to buy her. I still had time since Christmas was a month away.

"Will you quit being so slow moving," Penny said as I was daydreaming about what to buy her.

"I'm sorry, but I was just thinking something," I replied.

"Well, stop thinking, it gets you in trouble."

I smiled and followed her to the company van with our packages in hand. I took the van because I knew Penny would fill it, and she did. We dumped our latest booty in and she turned to me and said, "We need to go to a baby store to get presents for little PJ."

I pulled out my Samsung Note 3 phone and brought up Google. I searched for baby stores around the city and said, "Babies "R" Us over on Rainbow Boulevard would do the trick." She agreed, so we drove there and she led the attack. After an hour of Penny checking out all the baby things, she picked out a few toys and necessities for Lynn and Deacon's baby.

Back at the van, we dumped everything in and drove home. Our puppy Willy was going crazy when I opened the door, so I took him out for a run and a dump. Penny was unloading the van and taking everything in the house.

I was standing on the lawn watching Willy fertilize a small patch, when I saw a car driving up the road. It was Will Trapper. He was spending a lot of time with his girlfriend Sam that I saw little of him around the office. That was fine with me, it wasn't like we all had to be at work. We were independent and could pick our crime investigations as we wanted. It didn't make Lacey happy, but she endured.

He pulled into the drive and Willy made a bee line to him as he got out.

"Hey, there's my namesake," he said as he picked up the tiny dog. "Jim, are you busy?"

"Penny and I just got back from Christmas shopping, but I'm done now. What's up?"

Trick or Treat Murders

"I got a call from an old friend of mine, old as in age. He asked if I could help him with a problem." He put Willy down and we walked to the porch to get out of the hot sun. Willy ran to the door waiting for us.

"Okay, what's the problem that I feel you want me to help with?"

"He's a Santa Claus for one of the local charitable organizations in the city and he has been getting death threats. Now, I can't imagine who'd want to murder Santa Claus, but he asked me to help him."

"The death threats started when?"

"As soon as he started to go out and ring his bell for money. He was getting notes in his pot mixed in with the money warning him to stop playing Santa or he'd regret it."

"Just saying he'd regret it, no actual death threat?" I asked.

"Well, not in so many words. But he's really worried. I can't imagine there's a Santa union that's muscling in on the Christmas bell ringing Santas. That would be a first for me. Or a mob wanting a cut of the money. I figure if we watch over the guy and see who is doing this, well, I thought in the spirit of

Christmas, you'd want to help." He grinned and waited for me to respond.

"Ho, Ho, No," I replied, with a bigger grin. "After the Trick-or-Treat killer, I'm done with holiday cases. Besides, Penny and I may go for a late Thanksgiving back home in Michigan. Just close family, and I know Penny would murder me if I got on a new case. See if Earl will help, he loves covert operations. He'd be happy to do surveillance on a Santa."

"You're getting to be a Scrooge in your old age," Trapper said with a laugh. "I thought I'd give you a shot at it first."

"Who's getting shot?" came a voice from the front door. It was Penny.

"Hi, Penny. I was just asking Jim if he'd like to protect the life of Santa Claus."

"Does Santa need protecting?" she said as she came out of the house and moved over to us.

"This one does. He's a friend of mine and he's been threatened. He asked me to help him."

Penny looked at me and said, "You'd let Santa get hurt? Why?"

"He's not really Santa, and Will can protect him. Besides, we had talked about going back to Michigan for a late Thanksgiving," I said.

"We can do that at Christmas, I'd prefer it. Now you need to save Christmas like you saved Halloween."

"But I didn't save Halloween. I didn't even save the killer," I said.

Penny turned to Trapper and said, "He'll help you, or he'll get a lump of coal in his stocking."

They both looked at me, I was being ganged up on, so what could I say, "Merry Christmas."

*

Continued in the book...

~~*~~

Jim Richards Family of Readers

Thanks to the following people who are now part of the Jim Richards Family of Readers. They have read a book or more and enjoyed them. They all volunteered to be included in the list. If you are a fan of the books, send me your full name and you will be included in future books. Send your name to murdernovels@bobmoats.com to be added here and on the website. (updated 3-28-14)

* Achim Feifel * Al Norris * Alex Wheatley * Alexandra Delporte-Wilkinson * Amy Tapia * Andrea Bryan * Anne Shepherd * Arianda Sugar * Arlene Markowski * Ashley Augustus * Audra Hall * Barbara Hughes * Barbara Sammons * Barbara Schuler * Barbara Zirger * Beth Donohue Plenskofski * Betsy Childress * Beth Gibson * Bill Sandy * Bill Tornquist * Billie-jo Collie * Boni J Rychener * Carl Bishopric * Carla Lewis * Carole Henderson * Carolyn Conroy * Carolyn Riddle-Linington * Cassy Bailey * Chad Hudson * Charlotte L Duran * Cheryl L. Everett * Cindy Ackley Nunn * Cindy Valstad * Connie Bancroft * Corinne Kay O'Daniel * Dana Robbins Chuchran * Dana Wichita * Danielle Monique * Darren Heald * Dave Travers * David Wilkinson * DeAnn Jannereth * Deanna Miller * Deb Breuker Balbo * Debbie Carter * Debbie White * Deborah Fartuch * Deborah Gauze * Deborah Sullivan * Dee King * Denise Freeman * Diana Carver * Dixie Beck * Donna Gould * Donna Thompson * Donny Minter * Doris Kight * Eddie Moore

Trick or Treat Murders

* Eric Walters * Felicia Annette Bradfield * Francine Menor * Gail Chesney * Georgiann Minster * George Conner * Greg Colucci * Hayley Rankin * Harold Garcia * Heidi Arnold * Irma Ranee Coy * Jacqueline Moss * Jan Kimball * Janice Schneider * Janice Spoor * Jennifer Redmond * Jessica Keown-Belous * Jim Beck * Jo Boguslaw * Jo Turner * Joanne Marie Turner * John Peiffer * John Wisbiski * Joseph Wauro * Joyce Stacy * Joyce Trifiletti * Judy Franklin * Judy Travers * Judy Padgett * Julie Heath * Junnahvee Benson * Karen Dahl * Karen Grams * Karen Higham * Karen Kaiser * Karen Meinburg Richwine * Karen Kirkman Parker * Karin Hawkins * Karin Vasvari * Kathleen Donohue Roesing * Kathleen Riddle-Wolfe * Kathy Hinds Moore * Kathy Jones * Kathy Mitchell * Katie Benzler * Kay Burns * Kelly Garcia * Ken Boggs * Keota Rodriguez * Kiera Mccarthy * Kim Estes * Kitty Stolle * Kristie Sciler * Kirsty Stanton * LaLonnie Scallen * Larry Morris * Leann Parr * Lenora Scales * Leslie Marie Jackson * Linda Forester * Linda Ingle Cox * Linda Kennerö * Linda Magill * Lisa Bower * Liz Gibson * Lorraine Wiman * Loretta Alexander * Lynda Bowles * Lynette Lawrance * LuAnn Louttit * Manny Rothman * Marcia Gibson DeWitt * Marie Calder * Marlene Bryan * MaryLouise Kramp * Mary Lynn Gross * Megan Atkins * Meghan Hyden * Melody Cannavan * Michael Carruthers * Michael Dinkens * Michael Vannoy * Michelle Burns-Mitchell * Michelle Pilcher * Micki Potter * Mike Moats * Mimi Baur * Myrna Hecht * Nadine Sutton * Natalie Quine * Neena Martin * O'Della Wilson * Pat Pollington * Pat Rohn * Patricia Jarmon * Patricia C Trezza * Patrick Barry * Paul Lawrance * Peggy Davis * Phyllis Bassett * Raylene Matheny * Rebecca Collins Besner * Renee Brumley * Reta Hanna * Reta Moats * Roberta Navarro-Harder * Sally Berneathy * Sally Hubler * Sarah Santos *

Bob Moats

Satka Nikc * Sharon E. Edwards * Sharon Mangini *
Sharon McMillon * Sheena Rawl * Sherry Amstutz *
Shirley Alvarez * Shirley Davies * Shirley Williams *
Stacie Rowe * Stephanie Conner * Steve Cullen * Susan
Haughton * Susan Hesse Adams * Susan Salomon *
Suzan K Chase * Taisha Cullum * Tamara Moore *
Tammy Castleberry * Tammy Lynn Wood * Ted Murphy
* Terri Atkins * Terri Creech * Terry Raab * Tonia
Rachael Riggs-Williams * Travis Fleury-Lopez * Twyla
Gawlas * Val Brooks * Walt Munsel * Yvonne Isakson *

Thank you to all these wonderful people.

Thank you for purchasing this book. I hope you enjoy it as much as I enjoyed writing it for my faithful readers. Please feel free to email me to tell me what you thought about my stories. I love hearing from the readers. I can be reached at murdernovels@bobmoats.com thanks again!

*